# A Tunnel in the Pines

by

Lucia Greene

North Country Press

**A Tunnel in the Pines**

Copyright © 2015 by Lucia Greene

Cover art by Sophie Connolly
Cover design by Luke Connolly

ISBN 978-0-945980-57-5
Library of Congress Control Number: 2015932304


North Country Press
Unity, Maine

To Nora, Sophie, Luke and Thom, with love.

And to the Silvermine gang who dug the first tunnel.

"It may be doubted whether there are many other animals which have played so important a part in the history of the world, as have these lowly, organized creatures."
                    --**Charles Darwin on earthworms**, 1881

Andrew and I are playing sardines in a big house one night with a bunch of our friends. The house is unfamiliar, I'm not sure who owns it or why we're there, but the closets and the hallways and the rooms just seem to be going on and on, endlessly. It's completely dark, there are no lights on, making it the perfect setting for sardines. That's the way the game is played, in total darkness, so that your hair stands up at the back of your neck and you're scared half out of your mind. That's part of the thrill.

My best friend, Andrew, is 'it', which means that when and if I find him I just silently climb in alongside and wait for the others to arrive. Side by side, like in a can, that's why it's called sardines. One by one you disappear, until eventually there will be one kid left alone looking for the rest of us--a spooky, weird feeling if you've ever been unlucky enough to be that kid.

Slowly I inch down one of the longest hallways, using my hands out front and feet against the sides for guidance. At the end of the hall, I bump into a wall, then feel around and discover it is actually a door. Turning the knob and moving forward, I stumble a little over the door frame but catch myself before falling. It turns out to be a large closet filled with coats and sweaters.

"Andrew, you in here?" I ask quietly, but of course the rules say that even if he is, he can't answer.

Pushing past some of the clothes, I sink deeper into the darkness. Suddenly, I touch plastic. I know it's plastic because it's smooth and cool and slippery and gives a little under my fingers. I run them slowly over the front and discover the teeth of a zipper that has been left open. Reaching inside I brush up against fur coats, which sway slightly on their hangers in response. Then, just as I'm about to give up and turn away, a hand shoots out and seizes mine, making me jump almost out of my skin and cry out.

"Shhhh! Get in!"

My heart is thumping wildly as I slip in alongside Andrew, relieved to have been the first to find him and be home safe. For *several minutes, we stand next to each other silently, each of us happy we have found the other.*

*"Good spot," I say.*

*"Took you long enough," he whispers. "Close the zipper."*

*"Huh?"*

*"The zipper. Zip it and it'll be harder to find us."*

*I squat down, feeling along the outside of the teeth until I reach the bottom, and it's difficult but I pull the thing up, stopping somewhere near the top.*

*"All the way, Wills."*

*"What?"*

*"To the top, close it. They'll never find us."*

*It's hard from the inside, but I manage to get the zipper closed, bringing it up to the very top from within the plastic bag.*

*"Where are the others?"*

*My face is pressed into one of the coats. I reach one hand up, hold the fur against my nose, and inhale. Mink, I wonder, or beaver?*

*"I have no idea," I mumble. "They were spooking around together downstairs, in the kitchen, and I told them the whole point of the game was to split up and look for you, solo."*

*"Probably chicken," Andrew says. "Afraid of the dark."*

*"Probably. But this is a great spot, they'll never find us here."*

*"Hope not."*

*I close my eyes because it's warm inside our plastic cocoon, with Andrew and me breathing and giving off body heat. The fur has a peculiar smell, sort of wild and musky at the same time. I bury my nose into one of the coats again and breathe deeply, thinking it smells just a tiny bit like my mother. The warmer it gets in here, the harder it is to concentrate.*

*Beside me, Andrew coughs twice.*

*"So, OK, where are they?" he asks, again.*

*I run my hand down the side of one coat, feeling the silky fur ripple beneath my fingers. I don't answer, because I don't want* to. I'm actually starting to feel sleepy. It's getting warmer, and a little stuffy. Someone should open a window or something. That makes me want to giggle, because of course there aren't any windows to open, but then I remember we're not supposed to make any noise and put my hand over my mouth so I won't blow our cover.

"Open it."

"What?" I hiss.

"The zipper. There isn't enough air in here. Open it a little."

"You're never happy," I complain. "One minute you're telling me to close the thing and the next you want it open."

I reach out and feel for the front of the bag, then run my hands along the zipper up to the top. It won't budge; the zipper is stuck and won't move. I work on it for a bit, trying to jamb the thing down with force.

"Can't," I say. "You try."

"We really need some air," Andrew says loudly, not caring if anyone hears.

"Shhhh, quiet!" It's annoying that just because he's getting freaked out he's going to blow our cover.

I shove over so he can have a shot at getting the zipper open. Part of me thinks it's warm and cozy, a perfect place to take a nap, and I almost don't care if he is successful. The other part says it is getting harder to breathe. Andrew is right. Maybe closing the zipper all the way to the top wasn't such a hot idea.

"Ughhh!" Andrew grunts as he wrestles with the top of the bag. "How can this thing not open?"

Suddenly it isn't funny, not being able to get out of this plastic tomb we've closed ourselves into. It's weird but I don't feel half as alarmed as I should be. I'm sure someone will find us, sooner or later. And for some reason I can't stop yawning.

"Will we smother to death?" I say.

If we don't get out, this seems possible. The other guys will never find us and slip inside to become sardines. We won't have won anything after all.

Instead of answering, Andrew sinks to the ground, breathing in quick, shallow gasps of air almost like a dog panting. I start banging wildly against the heavy walls, hoping to rip through them and free us. They move and buckle under my blows, but remain intact. Twice I nearly fall as I flail away at the plastic until I am exhausted.

"Help!" I cry into the dark sea of coats. "Somebody, anybody, let us out! Help!"

"We're stuck in here, they'll never find us," Andrew says in a strange voice. He's down on the floor now making sniffling noises. If I didn't know better, I'd say he's crying. It dawns on me that if anyone discovers us they'll find him in tears, bawling his eyes out like a baby. We'll never hear the end of it.

"Nice," I say. "You were the one who said to close this thing to the top, and now you're blubbering like a two-year-old. Suck it up."

Instead of answering, Andrew stops crying. I don't know, maybe he's stopped breathing too. I listen as hard as I can but don't hear a sound. Maybe he's cried himself to sleep. I slip down to the floor and wrap my arms around my knees. It's getting harder to breathe and I can barely keep my eyes open. It's amazing how closely sleep resembles death. The big difference is in the waking up.

# Chapter One

I'm just telling Andrew about last night's crazy dream when we hear something. We're upstairs in his family's hayloft, cleaning the place out so we can start a club this summer. From the heavy, clumping sounds we know it's got to be Strat Sherwood and my brother, Taylor. Strat wears real lizard cowboy boots from Arizona, red ones with blue bucking broncos on each side that make major noise when he walks. The boots have heels, too, making him even taller than he already is.

Andrew squats down and holds a warning finger to his lips. I crouch alongside and throw an arm across his back. We huddle together, listening. Andrew's heart is thudding wildly against his chest. If we're totally quiet maybe we stand a chance, but if those two come upstairs and find us it's all over. No sense having them know anything about our club plans until we're ready. We stay motionless, looking at the floor instead of each other. If we lock eyeballs we'll burst out laughing. Then we're as good as dead.

"Wills! Andrew! You girls up there?"

The stairs creak as Taylor balances on the lowest boards. We flatten out on the floor, soundlessly, as smooth and professional as if we're in a video game.

Neither of us moves. Aside from the pigeons cooing in their bins across the stairwell it's completely still. I stifle this incredible urge to burp, so all that comes out is a tiny rumbling noise. Andrew jabs my side with his elbow.

"Huh! Wills told me he was headed here," Taylor says. He snaps his gum, breaking the silence. "Said he and Andrew had some sort of secret mission."

Taylor laughs a little too loud, like maybe it wasn't so funny but what the heck. He wants Strat to know he thinks we're just a couple of losers.

Strat grunts.

"Wimp!" he booms in his deep voice. He takes one or two steps up, his red leather cowboy boots making serious noise against the wood.

Andrew and I lock eyes. Which one of us is he talking about? Strat spits on the barn floor, a big, wet, nasty sound he's perfected with years of practice. It's his trademark. He's been playing hockey on the school team and every game he hurls a big one onto the ice. Someday a guy's skate is going to get stuck in the nasty stuff and he'll go down on his face. It won't be pretty.

"Oh Wills!" Taylor calls out. "Little brother of mine!"

The stairs creak again under Strat's weight. Barney, the Wylers' horse, snorts and turns around in his stall. He grabs hold of his grain bucket with his teeth, pulls it away from the wall, and bangs it against the side of the stall a couple of times for fun.

"What was that?" Strat asks.

"Nothin'. Just the mule," Taylor says. Andrew narrows his eyes at the insult, but I shake my head. "Okay, so, what'ya wanna do? Keep looking for the runts?"

My brother's gum cracks as a bubble breaks, hopefully stretching right across his big mouth.

"Naw, they're not here, c'mon," Strat orders, and out they go.

The screen door bangs--then it's quiet. Andrew and I crawl across the floor to the window. We watch the deadly duo as they cross the pasture and open the gate. Strat spots a pigeon pecking at the dirt near the fence and aims a wild kick at it. After it flutters briefly into the air and moves off, he grabs a chunk of Barney's manure and hurls it, just missing him. This time the pigeon sweeps up in a graceful arc and disappears over the roof of the barn.

"Man," Andrew whispers. "That guy is a major creep."

When we can no longer see their backs we stand and give each other a high five.

"What'll we call it?" I ask.

Andrew stops dancing and stares.

"Call what?"

"Us," I say. "Our new club."

He pulls his bandana back down around his neck and wipes his mouth with the back of his hand.

"The name should mean something," I say, "but it should be classified secret."

He nods.

"Yeah, good point. Give me a while. I'll come up with it."

We start arranging some old wooden crates in a kind of circle so they can be used for seats. Since we need to decide which kids we'll invite to join we start making a list of possible candidates.

"Taylor, you, me, that makes three." Andrew holds up three fingers. "Adam Shapiro." He holds up a fourth and I nod. Adam is cool. He knows how to fish and promised he'd show me how to tie a fly someday. Only day he can't fish is on Saturday, Jewish Sabbath, but that's only a problem during the school year.

"Strat Sherwood," I say, "right?"

Andrew's face grows pink.

"You joking?" he shouts, turning both thumbs down. "Did you hear that guy talk about wimps? He was talking about us, Wills. You and me!"

He pushes up his shirt and makes a muscle, imitating Strat. Only Andrew's arm is scrawny and pathetic so we crack up.

Once we're back making our list it only takes a few minutes to come up with additional names. Andrew writes them down, putting stars next to sure bets and question marks next to the others. There are more question marks than stars. Taylor and Strat he puts at the bottom.

"Girls?" I ask.

We look at each other.

"Females?" I try again.

I can only think of a few candidates so I shut my mouth.

"OK, maybe Connie," Andrew says. "Let's vote on that later." Connie's my big sister. She runs interference for me all the time keeping Taylor off my back. If we're even considering

3

having Taylor and Strat in the club we'll need her. Andrew's a fan so he puts a star next to her name.

I look out the window again to make sure the goon squad hasn't returned. No sign of them. They're probably out terrorizing the neighborhood. Little kids and old ladies, the easy prey. Andrew comes up behind me and looks over my shoulder.

"I hate that guy," he sighs. I nod. Doesn't matter which one he's talking about, they're both animals. Andrew presses his mouth against one of the clean panes and breathes, leaving behind a small circle of white mist.

The pasture is empty except for some of Andrew's dad's pigeons circling high above the barn. I'm pretty sure this is going to be an excellent club, whatever we name it. And when those two come back looking for us, we'll be ready.

# Chapter Two

Mr. Shepley is just pulling the bus away from the front of the school on Monday when Andrew lurches down the aisle and throws himself into the seat next to me. He sits on one corner of my jacket so I yank it out from under him.

"Man!" he says breathlessly, "Close call. Almost missed it."

His book bag is wide open and a mess of books and papers are sticking out of the top. We lean together as the bus leaves the school entrance and moves out onto the main road.

Everybody's yelling and bouncing in their seats. We surge forward then fall backwards in unison as Shepley works the gears.

"No kidding. Where were you?"

Andrew hefts his bag off his shoulders and it falls down in the space between us. Two seats in front B.J. Harris, a year behind in school and mean to the bone, aims a rubber band at Andrew and shoots, catching him on the side of the head. Andrew is so excited at making the bus he doesn't even notice.

"Quit it, B.J.!" I holler.

I shoot the thing back and of course, I miss.

"Ha!" B.J. yells.

He twists his ears and sticks out his tongue, frog eyes bulging. B.J.'s got short, black, uneven hair that looks as if it hasn't been washed in months. The guy is pathetic. He is older than we are but has been held back a couple of times. It didn't do him any good, he still acts like a two-year-old.

"Listen," Andrew says urgently. "Wills!"

He tugs on my shirt and I turn away from B.J. to glare at him.

"What, Andrew, what?"

It irritates me that he totally missed the exchange with B.J. When Andrew gets intense, only one idea fits into his head at a time.

"I had the best nightmare last night!" he says. "It was unbelievable, wait till you hear."

I swing my head around to keep an eye on B.J. and his gang. They can't be trusted. Now they're harassing some younger kids in front of them and one of the girls looks scared, like she's about to bawl. Old Shepley is eyeing them in the rear view mirror. He's a nice guy but on the bus he has absolutely zero control.

When things get really bad Shepley pulls over to the side of the road and threatens us with a broom. He stands up and bangs it up and down on the floor. Sometimes he waves the broom over his head like a baton. He's never hit anyone with it, most times kids just laugh. They like to see how far they can push before he grabs that broom. We judge the severity of the ride by how many times Shepley uses it. This is looking like a two-broom ride already.

Now B.J. and friends are yanking on one girl's braids every time she turns to face the front of the bus. I swear, I wish Mr. Shepley would just bring that thing down on their heads hard, just once. It wouldn't hurt much and it sure would get their attention.

"Wills!"

Andrew gently places a hand on either side of my face and turns it toward him, pushing my cheeks forward and my lips out. I must look like some kind of deranged blowfish or something.

I knock his hands away. Sometimes Andrew gets very touchy, like now, when he wants my attention. The bus hits a bump in the road and we both fly up in our seats. Andrew flies a little higher than I do just for the thrill of it. Everybody yells. A group of kids up front shove over suddenly, knocking a third kid into the aisle.

"My dream," Andrew continues. "I got the coolest idea for our club from my dream."

Andrew claims he gets his best ideas from dreams. To him, nightmares are like free horror movies, only without the popcorn. I call him the dream machine. Every time he starts to tell me about one, in all its gory details, I have to change the subject or go crazy listening.

Suddenly I remember last week's nightmare and how it felt to be closed into that tight plastic space with no air. I never did tell Andrew. *Why did I pull that zipper up all the way just because he told me to?* So now I fill him in, talking about us being shut into the bag and not being able to breathe.

"That's stupid, Wills," he tells me in disgust. "We'd never do something that dumb."

I sink back into the seat.

"What do you want from me? It was only a dream. It's not like I could control the thing."

But Andrew's not really listening. He wants to talk about his dream because obviously it's more important.

"Worms," he insists, his face pressed up close to mine. "Millions of worms, twisting and turning and taking over our clubhouse."

"Did they wipe their feet at the door?" I joke, moving away slightly.

If Andrew leans any farther over he will land in my lap the next time Shepley takes a curve. Old B.J. will love that.

"Stat Sherwood came in and they crawled all over him. They devoured him, he was totally compost within minutes," he says, caught up in his own fantasy. "It was awesome! All that was left were those boots. A thousand red worms can eat a half pound of garbage a day, so getting rid of Strat was no problem!"

Andrew sags back against the seat and clutches his bag, his eyes luminous, shining with pleasure. I look at him. His face is flushed and his breath comes in shallow little gasps, like he has just been running or something. Apparently getting rid of Strat is pretty exciting stuff.

"You all right?" I ask, deciding to change the subject.

Andrew doesn't answer, he just coughs a little, leans his head back against the seat and closes his eyes.

7

"Worms are incredible creatures," he says, slowly and carefully as if I might not understand. "If a small portion of their tail is cut off, they can grow a new one. Amazing. But if you take more than a quarter from their front, they die. I know all about this stuff. I read some research a guy named Darwin did more than a hundred years ago. I'm doing a final science project for Mr. Abbot and need to do research. We've got to keep a journal and record our observations, so I'm building a worm farm. Abbot says if I work on it over the summer he'll give me credit next year."

Just what Andrew needs, extra credit in science. Last year he won the science award for some project he did on hydroponics.

"The only good worm is a headless worm," I offer, bouncing around a little just for fun.

The bus turns up Beecher Road so in about four minutes we'll reach my stop. Halfway up Beecher I see a black dog with a red collar sitting in the middle of a driveway. The bus door hisses open to let some kids off and the dog bounds forward to greet them, its tail swinging madly. It jumps up, placing big paws square onto the chest of the smallest kid, almost knocking him over. His mother, leaning against a car talking on her cell, doesn't even notice.

"So the worms start with Strat's head, only they eat too far, and bingo, before anyone can stop them, he's just a big, steaming pile of compost," Andrew continues with satisfaction. "He does a lot of moaning and writhing before he kicks. I'm telling you Wills, it was brilliant!"

Andrew twists sideways in our seat and stares at me. Sometimes he gets so intense about things he forgets to blink. It's like his brain is on overload. He's doing it now and since it kind of freaks me out I look out the window. The dog has grabbed a stick and he's ramming it against the kids, begging them to play. One of them clutches his knee and howls with laughter, his mouth a wide, dark circle of happiness.

"Did you hear anything I said?"

I shrug.

"Some of it."

"It's called regeneration, when some forms of life can grow new parts," Andrew says. "Worms can, people can't. Scientists have been doing research to find out how to promote regeneration in people. The research this guy Darwin did on worms back in the 1800s started it all. Back then people thought he was nuts but now they realize he was a genius."

I turn from watching the dog.

"Can't what?"

Andrew sighs.

"Regenerate. Grow new parts," he says patiently. "What I was telling you."

The bus is slowing down in front of my street so I get up and gather my stuff together. I look down at Andrew.

"You've flipped," I say quietly. "Worms are slimy, boring creatures and if you find them fascinating you're insane. Anyway, what's this got to do with our club?"

Andrew swings his legs to one side so I can get by. He's so excited about this regeneration business I don't think he heard a word I said.

"Meet me at our barn in a half-hour and I'll tell you," he says.

He grabs my arm as I move into the aisle and squeezes it. He is into this, big time.

"Promise?"

"Fine!" I snap, yanking my arm away. I jump over B.J.'s outstretched legs on my way out. Last week he tripped me this way. I'm not stupid enough to fall for it twice.

# Chapter Three

Thirty minutes later, after grabbing a snack, we meet in the barn and Andrew starts in right where he left off. I hand him one of the juice packs I snuck out of our fridge. My mother says they're wasteful. She only buys them for car trips because they create more garbage and cost too much.

"Why don't we just name the club the Annelids?" Andrew suggests.

He squeezes the juice pack too hard and some shoots out of the straw and catches him in the face. Neither of us moves to wipe it off as it trickles down his cheek like a big red tear.

"The what?"

"Annelids. A group of worms with sectioned bodies the earthworm belongs to."

"Nobody will know what it means," I protest.

I reach over and wipe his face with the bottom of my shirt.

"Exactly! And we don't want them to, remember? I've been reading about worms and keeping a journal. In old legends they used to be called 'dragons' or 'serpents'. Today we know a lot more about them. They swallow huge quantities of earth, using the digestible material as food, and then pass the rest out. I read they can bring something like 18 tons of finely ground soil per acre each year to the surface, making the soil better. The compost they produce is called 'black gold' it's so fertile. They actually do the earth an incredible amount of good. Charles Darwin said that worms have played a great role in the history of the world."

"You're back on that guy again," I say. Sometimes he's like a broken record. "Who the heck is Charles Darwin?"

Andrew takes a long sip of juice and doesn't immediately answer.

"*Was*, Wills, *was*," he says patiently. "Darwin *was* this biologist who studied worms a long time ago. He found out some amazing things and was the first one to talk about evolution."

"I've always thought of worms as fish bait and bird food, nothing more," I admit. "The Annelids, a bunch of slimy earth movers."

Andrew nods eagerly.

"Right! Small, but powerful. Earth movers with proportionally super powers. Capable of great things. Darwin said that for their size, worms actually possess great muscular power."

This time I nod.

"Kind of like us," I say, thinking of my brother and his hulking sidekick, Strat. "It's sort of gross, but it works. Maybe our mission can be trying to figure out what the name means. That'll be part of the mystery."

"Exactly," Andrew says again. His eyes are wide and he keeps blinking, hard. "You and I will know, the others will have to solve the puzzle. We can even invite Taylor and Strat. It will take them months to put all the pieces together."

We hear Barney clomp into his stall downstairs. A fly, caught in one of the windows, buzzes in angry circles against the glass.

"What if they Google it?" I ask.

Andrew smiles.

"I'm way ahead of you. They're too stupid to even do the research. They'll think Annelid is some weird name we made up."

"Excellent," I say. "It just might work."

Andrew rises and goes out into the pigeon coop. He returns with an old fish tank he plunks down onto the floor in front of us. I recognize it because the Wylers used to have tropical fish, but when Andrew was little he spent a lot of time experimenting with the temperature controls to see how much heat the fish could take. They went belly up, one by one.

"What's that for?"

"The Annelids," he answers. "You and I are going to get started and build a worm farm, right now. It's called vermiculture."

I wave my hands, because I'm not interested in big words and I'm afraid he's going to launch into another one of his lectures.

"It's called worm poop," I say.

"We'll keep it here, at least for the summer. They like moist temperatures between 65 and 80 degrees so this old barn is perfect. I have to do it for Abbot anyway, so I figured I'd keep a journal and enjoy the club at the same time."

"Good idea, but I don't know the slightest thing about building a worm farm."

Andrew smiles and puts one hand on my shoulder.

"I knew you'd say that, Wills," he says. "I researched it on the Internet. It's no big deal. We're supposed to use a plastic bin, but I don't have one so we'll use this. All we do is fill it with newspaper torn into inch-wide strips, wet those down, then feed the things organic kitchen scraps every couple of days. They like coffee grounds, chopped lettuce, and other vegetable peelings but no meat. They eat the junk then turn it into manure which makes the earth richer. It's incredibly potent stuff. We may have to buy some red wigglers to get started but the garbage is free. After we get this set up we'll go out back by Barney's manure pile and get some soil."

So we clean out the old fish tank, grab some shovels and then head towards the woods behind the pasture. Little clusters of wildflowers are scattered all around and the skunk cabbage near the stream is starting to unfurl. Andrew reaches down, pulls a worm out of the earth and holds it high over his mouth, letting it slide slowly along the far side of his face as if he's eating it.

"Nice!" I punch his arm. "Now tell me again how we're going to do this."

13

"Well, we can use the five layer technique—chalky soil, a layer of peat, then sand, then garden soil, and lastly a layer of leaves and grass— but I think using newspapers will be a lot easier."

"A layer of Pete?" I ask. "How does he feel about that?"

It's hard work putting some laughs into this job, especially when Andrew is in his Mr. Science mode and taking it all so seriously.

"Peat, you know, the stuff they sell in garden shops. My mother has some in her gardening shed. The only thing we have to remember is to keep it fairly moist."

We're just adding a bottom layer of moist black earth when Andrew grabs my arm and points. Taylor and Strat are heading into the barn. They turn and look behind them as if they're being followed, like they're some kind of spies or something.

"C'mon," Andrew says, jumping up.

Two dark wet circles on the knees of his jeans mark where he knelt in the damp manure.

"Are you crazy?" I yelp, but I stand too.

"Take one side of this and help," he orders.

We lift the fish tank and head slowly toward the barn.

"They'll find out about this sooner or later," Andrew says, "so it may as well be now."

"They'll kill us."

Taylor would sooner beat me up most days than talk. I still have bruises on my shins from when he let me have it with the whiffle ball bat a few weeks ago.

"Maybe, but I don't think so. They'll be too busy trying to figure out what we're up to. It's better to take them by surprise than to have them find out what we're doing on their own. And since between them they have a brain smaller than an Annelid, that'll take months!"

We're already laughing when Barney pokes his head out the stall door. He's wearing his fly hood, a weird green net contraption that covers his eyes and face and has big, pointy covers over his ears. He looks like a Halloween joke gone bad.

"So tell me, why were you even reading about Darwin?" I ask. "Is that what you do for fun?"

I reach under and grab the tank from the bottom. The thing is surprisingly heavy. I meant to check out this Darwin guy that Andrew can't stop talking about but keep forgetting. If Andrew won't tell me I'll ask my father. He'll give me grief because of course Darwin's some famous scientist and I'm probably the only one on the planet who doesn't know who he is.

Andrew holds a finger to his lips. The tank lurches sideways when he slides his hand out from under it.

"Tell you later," he whispers.

Silently we enter the barn, ready to take the enemy by surprise.

# Chapter Four

My 'keep out' sign is turned around on the door, facing in. Strat is sitting on one of the crates with his lizard boots propped up on another, a long piece of yellow straw dangling from his thick lips. He's busy picking dirt out from underneath his fingernails and flicking it on the floor. When Andrew and I enter holding the fish tank, Taylor leaps out from behind us and slams the door shut.

"Aha!" he yells. "Got you!"

Slowly and carefully we lower the tank down over by the windows and Andrew knocks the dirt off his hands.

"Hey guys."

"So this is your big secret, pretty sad," Taylor says.

Strat stops picking dirt from his nails and studies the tank.

"Welcome to our club," Andrew continues. "The Annelid Club. We've asked Adam and Pete and a few other guys to join. It isn't for everybody, though. Not for the fainthearted. You've got to be really tough to be a member. We're planning on having a secret mission so each member will have to pass a test to join."

When Andrew says 'test' Strat yanks his feet off the crate and sits up straight. The straw stops dancing.

"Test? What kind of a test?" he growls, only because of the straw his words have a slight lisp. Each time I hear Strat's voice I'm surprised at how deep it is. A slight shiver runs through Andrew and he crosses his arms to steady himself. We've never before been this close to Strat without fearing for our lives. One false move and we're screwed.

"That's what we're going to determine tonight," Andrew says slowly. "I've asked the others to join us here after dinner for our first meeting. There's a lot to decide."

Taylor crosses the room to one of the crates and kicks it, hard. It slides across the floor and bangs into the wall.

"Why should we want to join your lousy club?" he asks. "What's in it for us?"

Strat grunts in agreement.

"Nothing," Andrew shrugs, holding both palms up, "and everything."

I nod, but honestly, what does that mean?

"Our mission is going to be to unravel one of the deepest mysteries of nature," Andrew continues, "and we're planning on using scientific theory to do that. This isn't going to be just a place where we all hang out, wasting time. We've got more important things to do."

Andrew really has their attention now. Neither one has taken their eyes off him. Not only are they dazzled by his language, they're trying to figure out what he's getting at. It's brilliant. I almost clap my hands, but that would break the spell, so I sit on them instead.

"Whadda ya know about science?" Taylor demands, eyes like slits. Everyone in the room remembers last year's science competition win, so this seems like an unusually stupid question, even for him.

Andrew looks pleased. He walks over to the fish tank and squats down, placing one hand tenderly on each end.

"See this baby? It's a worm farm Wills and I are building. You feed them organic garbage and they multiply. We're going to breed worms, hundreds of them. They'll be the club mascots."

Taylor slaps his leg as if this is the funniest thing he's ever heard.

"Worm farm? That's rich!" he snorts. "Looks like an old fish tank to me. Figures you two would pick the lowest being on earth for mascots."

Andrew's mouth opens, then shuts, while my brother basically knocks himself out laughing. Suddenly Strat rises and crosses over to the tank, and Andrew backs off. Strat bends over, peers in, and cocks his head to one side.

"Yeah, okay. So where are they?"

"Where are what?"

"The worms. Where are the frigging things?"

"We haven't gotten them yet," Andrew answers. "We were just getting ready to go out and dig near Barney's manure pile when you guys showed up."

Nobody says anything for a minute while Strat examines the tank. He's only looking at a bunch of newspaper, dirt and leaves, but he acts like he's studying the Mona Lisa.

"Right," he says softly, and straightens up. "We'll do it. C'mon."

He jerks his head towards my brother and moves for the door. Taylor watches, confused.

"What the heck? I don't even like worms," he whines, but Strat is already headed down the stairs, his boots clumping heavily against the boards. The door squeaks once, then again before banging shut as my brother follows Strat out of the barn and into the pasture.

From his stall Barney lets out a giant snort. I swear, it sounds like laughter.

# Chapter Five

Andrew and I cross to the window and watch as my brother hurries across the grass, trying to keep up with Strat. Strat barks some kind of order to Taylor, who nods and yells up to us, only we can't hear. The window probably hasn't been opened in years so it takes a few good bangs before I pry it loose. Little pieces of the white stuff around the glass fall off as I raise it a couple of inches. The air rushing in is warm and sweet.

"How many?" Taylor calls.

He holds up both hands. The guy still counts on his fingers, it's sick.

Andrew cups his hands around his mouth.

"About fifteen," he yells, "that'll do it."

"Hey," I say, "thought we had to buy the worms, those red wigglers, right?"

"Yeah, but they don't know that. Don't spoil their fun, Wills. Let them keep busy digging, it gives them something to do besides harassing us."

Strat strides off and Taylor has to run to catch up. Andrew and I sink to the floor. He starts giggling and I join him. Pretty soon we're laughing so hard I get a shooting pain in my side and Andrew's rolling around, clutching his ribs.

"It worked!" he gasps. "They took the bait. They're in."

I shake my head.

"Unbelievable! We only have one problem, what's our mission going to be? You told them we had one and all we really have is an empty fish tank and a little dirt."

Andrew stops rocking and takes a deep breath. He leans against the wall, his eyes shut.

"I have no idea," he admits. "I just said that to throw them. But relax, we'll figure something out before tonight's meeting."

"I thought the big idea came to you in last night's dream," I say. "Didn't the great God of nightmares pay a visit?"

He opens his eyes and looks straight ahead. Then he smiles. "Actually, last night I dreamt about a girl."

I glance sideways to see if he is kidding, but he's not. He's sitting there, head against the wall, hands folded, a truly goofy expression on his face.

"Sick," I moan, "that must have been a killer nightmare."

He opens his eyes and stares down at his hands, hard, like maybe something is written there.

"Which one? Which other did you dream about?" We've always called girls 'others'; it's our code name.

"Connie."

It takes me a minute to think about what he just said, and then his strange expression tips me off.

"Connie my sister?" He nods. I look at him, ready to laugh and share the joke, until I realize he isn't kidding.

"I was in the hospital, very sick, dying really, and she was my doctor. She saved my life."

Andrew has always taken his dreams very seriously so this one is no exception. It's clear he really believes my sister saved his life, that this is some sort of transforming experience. Sometimes he's just too weird for me to take. This is one of those times. I lunge forward, grab him by the shoulders, and shove hard till he falls over. His head just misses the edge of the tank.

"Hey!" he yells.

I'm so disgusted I don't even wait to see if he's okay. I stand up and move toward the door. Andrew stays on the floor, motionless. It's surprising how good it felt to knock him down.

"Put your measly worms to bed and tuck them in," I say. "I'll see you around seven."

Without speaking, he gets to his feet and brushes the dirt off his jeans. We haven't had many fights during our friendship and now he won't even look at me. Just before going out, I pick the club sign off the floor. It is kind of stupid, maybe I'll pitch it.

"Oh yeah, one last thing, dream machine," I say. "Leave my sister out of this, okay?"

Andrew grabs the bottle of Windex and hurls it, but I slam the door just as it hits, taking the stairs two at a time just in case he's in pursuit. Outside I almost crash into Taylor and Strat with their shiny little bucket of worms. They look ridiculous, like a regular pair of Jack and Jills. Taylor throws a quick punch at me just out of habit.

"Wills," Strat says. I realize it's one of the few times I can remember him actually using my name. "So, what do worms eat, anyway?"

He is totally taken with this worm stuff, right up there with Andrew.

"Worm food," I almost shout, but don't, because I'm pretty sure I can't outrun him. Just behind Strat's head I see the sun going down. The chorus of peepers over by Wyler's pond is sending its sweet, crazy song into the darkening sky.

"Ask the expert!" I yell and start running.

Behind me I hear Taylor in pursuit, his breathing hot and heavy as he chases me all the way down the path and into the darkening woods.

# Chapter Six

"Ma," I announce at dinner, "I'm heading over to the Wylers' at seven for a little while."

My mother is in the middle of giving my father seconds. Dinner is great, a pasta, crab and artichoke casserole and I've already had two helpings. I hate the way my mother waits on my father. He sits at the table, silently, as if his legs are broken. I glance at Connie but she's busy getting salad. Taylor has his mouth so crammed with food it's oozing out the corners. There are dark stains on the front of his tee shirt from last night.

My father studies me from behind his glasses and reaches for his wine. He loves good food and wine, so this is the high point of his day. I count the artichoke hearts remaining on his plate and wonder if he isn't going to eat them, can I.

"Have you done all your homework, Wills?" he asks.

"Yeah," I say. "I have one last science project so I was thinking…"

"What did you get on that math test last week?"

He doesn't wait to hear about my project, he just wants to know about my grades. My dad is a results kind of guy. It isn't how you get there, it's what you get when you arrive.

"I don't know," I lie, "we haven't gotten them back yet."

The truth is, I didn't get a good grade but I don't feel like announcing that to the family. Connie looks over and smiles in sympathy. She has probably done the same thing a zillion times.

"What's going on over at Wylers'?" my mother asks.

She's seated again and just kind of pushing her food around on her plate. My mother is a really pretty woman, she was definitely a babe when she was young. Now her dark hair is streaked with gray and small lines frame the corners of her eyes from smiling so often. It's my mission to get her laughing as often as I can.

Taylor has finally polished off every speck of food on his plate and decides to rejoin the human race. He stretches his big feet out under the table, knocking them into mine. I push back as we press the soles of our feet together in silent struggle. I put my fork down and hold on to the sides of my chair for strength.

"Me and Wills and Andrew have started a little club," he says, a little too loudly because he is pushing against me with all his might.

"Andrew, Wills and I," my father corrects. "English is your first language, and you children are old enough to speak properly."

"Yeah, whatever," Taylor shrugs.

My father looks at him across the table. He is probably wondering where this moron of a son came from. Taylor straightens up abruptly and yanks his feet away.

"What kind of a club?" my mother asks.

I slide my feet under me, push back the chair, and get up to clear my plate.

"A science club," Taylor answers quickly, flashing me a grin.

"Aha, science, wonderful," my father says. "Learn something while you're having fun. That's a good idea."

Taylor certainly has a knack for telling the man what he wants to hear, even if it bears no resemblance to the truth. He does this with teachers, too. They love it.

Now he turns halfway towards me, puts his hand to his forehead, and winks. My parents are both smart people but sometimes the stuff they fall for is unbelievable. Connie snorts in disbelief and shakes her head.

"A *science* club?" she asks.

She probably thinks we're going to recreate Frankenstein in the Wylers' barn.

"Yeah," I say. "Our first meeting is tonight. It'll only take about an hour. We should be home by eight."

"Fine," my mother says. "As long as you've both done your homework I guess it's okay."

Taylor and I get up to help clear the table, and afterwards start over to Andrew's. I beat Taylor out the back door so he gives me a hip check, hard, slamming me against the side of our garage.

"Race you there, butthead!" he shouts and races off.

I take my time, partly because I don't want him to think I'm trying to catch up but mostly because my side hurts. Having Taylor involved in this club is not making my life any easier. By the time I reach the barn the rest of the guys are already there. I say hello to Barney on my way in. He's so busy eating hay he doesn't even look up.

"Wills," Andrew says when I open the door and enter.

He's sitting on a crate in the middle of the floor, and six or seven kids, including Strat and Taylor, are seated around him. All the crates are taken, so I just stand there.

"Take a seat big guy," Taylor says sweetly, and laughs.

Andrew jumps up and disappears into the room with the pigeons, returning with a dirty crate. He kind of drops it down, casually, but I know it's for me.

"Thanks," I say, without looking at him.

Even though I'm still mad about the Connie thing, we always stand united against the enemy. Adam and a black kid named Colin, new to the neighborhood, say hello. Pete Wong, who lives on the other side of the Wylers, is seated in front of the worm farm, peering in. Andrew must have gone ahead and invited him without telling me. Pete is kind of a goofball, but Andrew likes him. He's really smart--somebody at school told me he's already taking pre-calculus. His dad teaches with mine in the physics department.

Pete wears black, heavy rimmed glasses and is skinny and sort of funny looking. Andrew calls him an idea man, whatever that means. Right now he is picking nervously at some zit on his neck, and from the looks of it, he has already taken care of the ones on his face. I just know Taylor and Strat are going to make Pete's life miserable. The way I see it, we don't need brains to deal with those two, we need bodyguards.

"Ok, c'mon, let's get moving, I've got stuff to do," Strat growls.

The lizard boots are stretched out in front of him and it looks as if he is about to slide right out of his chair. His big, hairy arms are crossed over his chest, muscles bulging and sleeves rolled up to expose them. I keep an eye on the top button of his shirt, which looks ready to pop off and fly across the room at any minute.

"Right," Andrew says, and clears his throat. He has a pad and pencil on his lap as if he is going to take notes. "This is the Annelid Club's first meeting. We're going to be democratic and vote on things so everybody has a say." He glances over at Pete, who nods at him. "Those worms over there are our mascots. They're epigeic worms, commonly known as red wigglers--hard working and ambitious, they're actually very powerful creatures. I realize they probably don't look impressive to you guys, but I promise that after hearing about them you'll change your minds. The more you learn the more amazing they become."

All of us turn towards the fish tank, and a few kids laugh nervously. One slimy, fat worm is pressed up against the glass doing absolutely nothing. In fact, it looks dead. As a mascot he's hardly inspiring.

"We shouldda picked the slug," Taylor says, "then we couldda been called The Slug Club."

We all crack up, even me, because really, this does seem sort of ridiculous. There is absolutely nothing going on in that tank. Andrew just sits there, face flushed, looking intense.

"Let's vote on membership," Taylor suggests.

He's probably planning to vote me out.

"Yeah," Andrew says. "Good idea. I don't think we should have any more than ten members to start, and we've got seven now. If anyone has any suggestions, write them down and we'll vote at the next meeting."

"Dues?" Adam asks.

Andrew nods.

"How much?"

"I'm not sure. Wills and I thought about a couple of dollars, what do you guys think?"

"Sounds reasonable," Taylor says, "but what will we use the money for? More worms?"

He snorts and claps Strat on the back but Strat doesn't even crack a smile. I'm happy to see that Taylor is starting to get on Strat's nerves. It is nice to have company.

Suddenly, Pete raises his hand above his head. The guy must think he's still in school. Andrew nods in his direction.

"Why don't we save up for a laptop?" he asks eagerly. "We could do some research on worms, maybe raise and sell them to make some money."

His voice rises and kind of hangs there, as if he's asked a question. Taylor, Adam and Colin make rude noises, and Pete's face flushes pink.

"We'll decide and vote on that, too, at another meeting," Andrew says quickly. "Right now it's important to decide what our mission will be and what we'll do for the club's initiation rites."

"Huh?" I say. "Initiation rites?"

He's way beyond me on this one. I thought we'd just vote on people we wanted in the club and they'd become members. I thought the test stuff was just a goof. That was something we'd use to psyche out Taylor and Strat, you know, demoralize the bad guys. Andrew's managed to pull a fast one on everybody, including me, and I'm as clueless as they are. For an inside guy, I'm way outside the loop.

# Chapter Seven

"What initiation?" Colin asks.

Andrew leans forward on his crate, hands on his knees.

"To determine who is strong enough to become an Annelid, and who isn't. Separate the men from the boys, the weak from the strong. Looks can be deceiving, guys. Consider the lowly earthworm, capable of changing the face of the earth. Our initiation won't only test physical power, it will gauge mental strength as well. There has to be a test, all great clubs have one."

Andrew is into this, big time. He's been watching too many Superman movies or something. He's not your typical macho type, but he sure is trying. Strat leans forward and cracks his knuckles.

"Yeah," he says slowly, "excellent. Let's make it really, really tough, so not everybody passes. Weed out the weak, the unwanted. No wimps allowed."

Almost every kid in the room thinks Strat is talking about him. Pete looks like he is about ready to pee in his pants. He probably thought he was joining a simple club, not a Marines ground unit.

"It needs to be something really challenging," Taylor says, his face screwed up from the effort involved in thinking. "Something wild."

He runs his tongue around his lips the way he does when his brain is smoking. I have visions of us scaling a mountain, Everest maybe, the Annelid Club flag at the top, waving and snapping in the breeze.

"Like what?" I ask, looking toward the tank for inspiration. One of the worms has made a channel, a little narrow corridor of dirt running alongside the glass. If everyone else thinks this initiation stuff is okay then who am I to resist? All of a sudden it hits me.

"How about we dig a really deep tunnel and make like the worms do, join our powerful brothers underground?"

I press my hands together and wiggle my body. I'm being totally ridiculous and they're all watching me. As soon as I begin my gyrations I know I've made a big mistake. Instead of taking it as a joke, Andrew's face lights up. He looks as if he's just won a million dollars. Strat claps his hands as Taylor punches his right fist into the air.

"Yes! That's it!" Andrew shouts. "Wills, you're brilliant. We'll dig a tunnel deep into the earth, just like the mighty worms do. That's the perfect Annelid mission."

I look around the room in total surprise. Everyone--Pete, Adam, Colin, even Strat and Taylor--is grinning at me. Strat extends his hand and I quickly take it, not sure whether he's going to flip me or shake it, but afraid to leave it there too long in case he changes his mind.

"We'll carve a secret chamber room into one end of the tunnel," Taylor says, eyes shining. "It'll be our initiation chamber and we'll have to crawl to get there. Anyone who can't make it through won't become a member."

They all start talking at once and I realize it's too late to tell them I was being sarcastic, making a joke. Connie always says sarcasm is the lowest form of humor, and this is as low as it gets. Even Andrew has gotten sucked in. He is up on his feet with the rest of them, jumping around and acting like a nut. I hide my face in my hands but Taylor and Andrew come over and pull me to my feet. Strat comes up too, so close I can see the fine hairs in his nose. Mr. Abbot once told our class they act as tiny filters, weeding out the dust and grit. Right now Strat's are working overtime.

"Wills, my man!" he booms. "Who wouldda thought?"

He grabs my hand again, and this time almost crushes it to the bone. The pain is so intense my knees kind of buckle and I twist sideways in agony, but the big brute doesn't notice a thing. He just releases me, turns around, and holds up his hand for everyone to stop talking. All of a sudden he's directing the show, the master of ceremonies.

"Let's get going right away, we'll start this weekend," he announces. "Bring shovels, pitchforks, axes, anything you've got for digging. It's gonna take some time, but this tunnel will be totally awesome!"

We all get up and exchange fist bumps. I try to miss Taylor's fist, but he connects with mine, hard. Now that we have a shared mission, we're best buddies. Strat and Taylor head for the door. They've practically got their arms around each other, and I swear, my brother is almost skipping. I slide over next to Andrew. He has his back towards me, facing the window.

"Nice going," I say. "Now they're in forever. Was that really wise?"

It takes him a moment to turn around. When he does, he gives me an odd look.

"Why not, Wills?" he asks. "What are you afraid of?"

I don't answer because I don't really know. The night is suddenly so chilly I shiver. I squat down next to the tank and peer in. Andrew's told me that worms are nocturnal creatures so this is prime time. One of them has tunneled down alongside the edge, barely moving, his body undulating forward slowly in convulsive little jerks. It looks like a lot of effort for very little gain. When we dig our tunnel it isn't going to be easy, though I guess I really don't know. I have no idea how to dig a tunnel but neither do any of these guys.

"You're not chickening out, are you Wills?" Andrew's voice floats down, but I don't take my eyes off the worm. "Because it was your idea, right? And it's a brilliant one, really, when you think of it, the perfect initiation. The big guys ate it up."

The worm continues its painfully slow journey along the side of the tank.

"Why do we call a creep a 'worm'?" I ask, not really expecting an answer.

An earth tunnel, not built by worms but by humans, as deep and long as we have the strength to dig it. Maybe it isn't such a bad idea after all. It will be dark, very dark, ideal for worms but not so hot for people.

"Pete!" I yell.

He's just gone out the door, but hears me and comes back in.

"Think you can do a little research on tunnels, how the good ones are dug and all that?"

He blinks hard and nods.

"Sure, Wills."

I turn back to the tank. "We'll need some directions," I say softly, "We'll need a plan. It's not going to be that easy to dig this tunnel."

"No problem," Pete says.

He's happy I've asked for help. Research is his specialty. Andrew says he spends most of his time in the library, so I'm pretty sure he's up to the job.

"Strat and Taylor kind of took over on this thing. That wasn't part of the deal."

I glance at Andrew. Some of his fine white hair is sticking up in the back. Against the light it looks like a halo. He shrugs.

"I'm worried about that," I admit. "We only wanted to stump them, to stay one step ahead in the puzzle, to not have them take control. That kind of backfired. This initiation stuff could turn out to be a disaster."

"Hey," Andrew says, "relax. I think you're being a little dramatic. I've got a plan. We just need those guys to do the grunt work, we don't need them for brain power. Let them break their backs digging this thing while we run the show."

Pete remains standing, looking first at Andrew, then at me, like we're at some kind of ping-pong match or something. He blinks and nods the whole time Andrew is talking.

"Okay, but I hope your plan includes making it through this initiation alive. I hope you know what you're doing," I say. "And one other thing, Strat wanted to know what worms eat."

"They like leaves, carrot shavings, vegetable peelings," Andrew says. "They'll eat garbage. Darwin discovered that sometimes they even eat small stones to help push stuff through their digestive systems. Actually, a bunch of old ladies in New York City put them in their apartment closets and feed them scraps for compost. Worms have an amazing capacity for survival, which explains why they've lived for thousands of years."

I study the tank. The worms look pretty mellow. They don't really look as if they have much of a capacity for anything, really. But if I say this to Andrew, he'll launch into another one of his lectures about Darwin's research on the incredible earthworm. And tonight I just don't want to hear it.

Suddenly, I'm tired. I stand and stretch, then bend over to tie one of my sneakers. The only light in the room is a bare bulb hanging in the center. A few moths are circling it, banging furiously into its seductive white glow. The room is silent. Everybody has left except Pete, Andrew and me.

"I seriously hope we survive this club," I say to no one in particular, heading for the door.

Andrew laughs as if I've said something really funny.

"Lighten up, will you Wills? You wanted some excitement this summer, right? I'm just trying to deliver. Consider this the biggest adventure of our lives."

I nod, say goodbye, and go down the stairs and out into the night. It's been raining lightly, and the earth smells rich and mysterious, as if maybe it holds some deep, dark secrets. I can just barely make out the path home because most of the moon is hidden behind clouds.

I've got questions for Pete. Where will we build the tunnel, and how deep and long should it be? Are we going to be able to breathe in there? How are we going to make it strong enough to support a roof? Andrew and I wanted to have an amazing summer, but we may be way in over our heads with this one. I have a scary feeling we've started something that'll be impossible to stop.

# Chapter Eight

When I wake up Saturday morning it's raining. A layer of heavy fog hangs suspended above the ground like a blanket of clouds. After Connie and I eat breakfast, she follows me into the basement, curling up on the couch while listening to her iPod as I shoot hoops. Taylor plays a lot of basketball so my father put a net on the far wall. Our ceilings are pretty high but it's still low, not regulation height, and I can actually sink some in.

"So," Connie says, "what's the deal? Taylor told Dad you guys started a science club, but we both know that's crazy."

I race across the floor, leap out of reach of the outstretched arms of the imaginary opposing team, and push the ball through the hoop.

"Sweet!" I yell, because this is a rare moment for me. The only time I'm any good at this game is when nobody else is around to challenge the play. I dribble hard in a few tight victory circles before I answer.

"Oh, that. Taylor kind of goofed on Dad when he said that," I tell her. "It is just a club in Wyler's barn that Andrew and I got going. Taylor and Strat crashed their way in and are taking over."

"For real?" Connie says. "Aren't they a little old to be hanging around with you and Andrew. Who else is in it?"

"Adam Shapiro, this new kid, Colin and Pete Wong. We haven't figured it all out yet, we still need a few more members. The big guys are only included so they won't terrorize us. We're thinking they'll get bored and drop out, but not before they've done some of the hard stuff that needs to be done."

Connie leans her head back, closes her eyes, and sings along with her music. I practice dribbling, moving and spinning and trying to control the ball as I weave around the floor. Andrew should be here. He loves hanging around my sister, it's beginning to annoy me.

Sometimes I have a creepy feeling he comes over to see her instead of me. I hurl the ball toward the hoop, badly, and it crashes against the rim and ricochets off, landing near Connie's feet.

"Hey, Wills, take it easy," she says, raising her voice above the music and tucking her feet up under her on the couch.

"Sorry."

"You don't really want Taylor and Strat in your club," Connie says. "So you have two options. Either make it so dull and boring they drop out, or so mentally challenging that you leave them in the dust."

I nod. My father claims that in this age of political correctness nobody is plain out dumb anymore, just mentally challenged. That would include Taylor.

I fly down the court, turn, twist, and slam the ball in again.

"Right, we're way ahead of you," I grunt. "That was basically our plan. I think Andrew is a little afraid to try and get rid of them, especially now, but you know Taylor, he gets such pleasure out of making my life miserable."

"It's sad," Connie says with a laugh. "And Strat," she continues, reaching back and drawing her thick hair into a ponytail. She yawns deeply and we both crack up, as if the thought of him is too exhausting for words.

"I think the big guy has the hots for you."

I carefully avoid looking at her and concentrate on the ball.

Connie knows this already. Everybody around them knows it. Strat practically stutters whenever she's in the room. He flexes his mighty muscles and gets very loud, even more obnoxious than usual. It must be some kind of ancient mating ritual, I have no clue. It's so painful I almost feel sorry for the guy.

"Please, don't make me heave," Connie says, yawning again. "I'm sitting for the Kapoors today at two. I hope they stay out a long time so I make lots of money."

"Better wear your armor," I warn. The Kapoors run a restaurant in town. She always comes home smelling like Indian food and the last time she sat for them one of the twins threw up all down her back.

I try for a second long shot down the court, taking time to set it up. The minute the ball leaves my hands I'm positive it isn't going in, but I'm wrong. It hits the rim, rolls around the edge for a split second, and then drops down neatly through the net.

Connie whistles.

"Wow. I think you're improving, Wills," she tells me.

I feel a surge of happiness.

"Really?"

"Yeah. A few months ago you wouldn't have come close on that shot. I see definite improvement."

She's right, I know. I decide to get down here more often for practice, once a day at least. Maybe if I do that I'd be decent and could even try out for the team next year.

The basement door swings open and light streams down the stairs.

"Wills! Phone!" my mother calls.

"Thanks, Ma. Who is it?"

I toss the ball into the trunk filled with sports stuff.

"I don't know. Didn't recognize the voice."

"See ya," I say to Connie. A loaf of apple bread is baking in the oven so the kitchen smells good. When I answer I work at making my voice deeper than usual.

"Hello?"

"Wills?"

"Is that who you called?"

There's a brief silence while the person on the other end tries to figure this out.

"Yes, hi Wills, um, it's Pete. For a second it didn't sound like you. I did a little work on this tunnel thing, some drawings, and I've got something to show you and the guys. Can you meet me over at the club?"

"Yeah, fine," I say. "Should we call Andrew?"

"Already did. He'll meet us there in a half hour."

"Dude," I say to close the deal.

"Excuse me?"

Even if I'd never met Pete, I'd be able to tell from his voice that he's a goof. One of those kids who unfailingly pleases teachers and parents. He's kind of out there, like he operates on a different wavelength or something. My dad has a theory that guys like Pete are the rocket scientists of tomorrow. He may be right.

"Fine," I say, "meet you there."

Before leaving I grab a thick slab of my mother's bread, still warm. She wraps a piece for Andrew, one for Pete, and hands them to me.

"Thanks. You'll make Andrew a very happy man."

"Give him my regards," she says, and kisses the top of my head. "Remember that your father is taking you for a haircut at three. Be home in plenty of time."

The last time we set this up I forgot and came home an hour late. It wasn't really a big deal, the barber took us anyway, but my dad was ticked off and I was grounded for a week.

"Yeah, right," I say, "thanks for the reminder."

On the way over to Wyler's the path through the woods is muddy so I can't run as fast as I'd like. Even though the fog is thinning, the trees are dripping like crazy. I dodge their bullets pretty well but I'm still wet by the time I arrive, panting, at the barn. Barney is totally soaked and the place smells like wet horse.

"Barns," I greet him. "How's breakfast?"

Barney raises his big head from the hay and swings around to look at me. When I reach my hand out he pushes his soft nose against it, his lips searching for a treat. Finding nothing he lowers his head and goes back to his meal. I take the stairs up to the loft two at a time, eager to view Pete's plans so we can get started on this tunnel.

# Chapter Nine

Andrew and Pete are already there, kneeling down over drawings spread out on the floor.

"Awesome," Andrew says when he sees me come in. "Wills, you gotta see this!"

I throw my jacket on a crate and join them. Pete's drawn plans for the tunnel on a giant piece of heavy white paper and coffee cans filled with pigeon feed are holding the edges down. He's supplied dimensions, not only for the tunnel itself but for the room at the end and its opening. He shows the tunnel from above, from the side, and a cross section of what the interior walls will look like. There's even a small scale in the lower left hand corner, one inch equals a foot. The exterior surrounding the tunnel shows woods and a stream, as if he already has imagined where we'll dig. It actually looks magical and slightly unreal, like something out of a fairy tale.

I whistle softly and rock back on my heels.

"Nice," I tell Pete. "Impressive."

He squirms, pushes his glasses a little further back on his nose, and turns pink.

"Actually, the only hard part was drawing the roof," he admits. "We're going to have to use wide boards, and cover them with dirt and grass and stuff as a kind of camouflage. That might work."

"What if some jerk comes through the woods and steps on it?" Andrew asks. "Will the thing cave?"

"If we use plywood it should hold up. That stuff is stronger than it looks."

I turn to Pete and wave my hands over the plans.

"Seriously, how'd you draw these?"

"Charcoal pencils," Pete says. "It was simple once I figured out what the dimensions should be. It's not going to be that easy to dig but I'm pretty sure we can do it."

Suddenly, we hear a rustling noise downstairs. Andrew presses a finger to his lips.

"Strat?" he whispers.

We freeze, alert to even the smallest noise. Pete looks at me and blinks.

"Relax," I say, "just Barney lying down."

I pass around the bread my mother sent. Andrew takes his and wolfs it down, so fast he starts coughing. So I clap him on the back several times just for fun.

"Stop!" he mumbles, stepping away from me. "So when are we going to dig this and where?"

Crossing over to the window, I bend down to check out the action in the tank. The worm that was up against the side last night has moved so there's basically nothing to see but dirt.

"How about your woods," I say, "somewhere in the pines near that big rock pile? Maybe we should all try to meet tomorrow if it doesn't rain."

Now that the plans are ready I'm anxious to get started. We need to get going, get this thing moving forward. If we spend too much time fooling around, the tunnel and the club may never happen. "How's your worm diary going?"

Andrew had said he was going to keep a diary, record the care and feeding of the worms along with their reproduction rates. Still, it's kind of low of me to bring it up in front of Pete. A diary isn't cool, it's something girls keep, not guys, but hey, Pete's the only one here. It's not like he'd know the difference.

"Journal," Andrew nods. "I'm keeping notes in a journal. I found out that worms are invertebrates, which means they don't have backbones, but that annelids are kind of the sophisticates among them because they have digestive tubes, circulatory systems, and brains. Darwin discovered they breathe through their skin, which is so sensitive they can actually feel a bird as it lands on the ground."

Before I can help myself, I snort out loud. Andrew is getting heavy about worms again. When he starts dreaming about worms with brains, we're in trouble.

"Jeez, how do they pack all that stuff into those skinny, slimy bodies?" I ask. "Did Darwin say anything about that?"

Immediately Andrew's face grows stormy. He gets up.

"What's your problem?"

I look up at him without answering and just smile, knowing it drives him wild.

"You know what it is with you, Wills?" he sputters.

Pete keeps his eyes on the floor because clearly, he doesn't like the way this conversation is going. He rolls up the plans and slips a rubber band around them.

"You and Taylor have a very limited attention span. Things get too deep, too complicated, and you guys blow them off! You're just like your brother. You can't handle it."

"Ouch," I say, unhappy to be lumped in with Taylor. "I only asked about your little diary, Andrew, not for details from the slimy underworld."

I glance at Pete and laugh, willing him to join in, but he keeps his eyes glued to the plans, sliding the rubber band up and down his master drawing, without looking at me. I know I'm being a creep but I can't stop. The only thing I can do is go forward.

"Get a life," I say to Andrew. "Writing notes in your precious little book about earthworms can hardly be fascinating. One of them moves half an inch and it's a major event."

I hook my thumbs in my jean pockets and smile again at Pete, who looks over briefly then quickly away.

Andrew goes nuts. He balls up the piece of foil my mother used for the bread and hurls it, catching me on the side of my face.

"Ow!" I yelp, "I'm wounded! Help! Dial 911!"

I pitch over onto my side, clutching my ribs, howling in mock pain.

"Jerk!" Andrew says to Pete. "C'mon, we're out of here."

They leave, taking Pete's plan. Andrew slams the door behind them. All I can hear is my own breathing. From where I'm lying I see the sun fighting to emerge from behind a cloud. The bottom is dark, but the top, where the sun is about to surface, is a brilliant silvery white, so blinding it almost hurts to look. Above it a pale rainbow has formed. I wonder if Pete and Andrew, crossing the pasture, notice.

After a minute I get up, brush myself off, and look around for the dues box. Somebody is going to have to keep track of the money, since it isn't beyond Taylor and Strat to dip into our cash for extra spending money.

I search in all the crates, behind the burlap sacks, even check out the pigeon room. I can't find the box, but I do find a small, loose-leaf notebook with a blue cover hidden alongside one of the nests. I wipe a cluster of gray feathers off the back before opening it.

"Easy, girls," I tell the birds.

Their small, shiny heads gleam in the sun and they keep their beady eyes fixed on me, like I'm some kind of criminal. The last thing I need is for some mother pigeon to think I'm going for her eggs and attack.

On the front of the notebook Andrew has written, The Worm Diary, in neat, careful script. Sinking into the straw, out of reach of bird droppings, I thumb through the pages. Andrew has recorded each stage of our Annelid Club, how it started, who joined, even how the two of us set up the worm farm. I read some personal things, stuff about Strat, Taylor and school. He even has the thing about the dream starring Connie in there, including my anger over it. I don't like reading about his dream any more than I liked hearing it, but at least he doesn't come out and declare his love for my sister.

Then I read something surprising.

*'Went to the doctor today. Brady did a bunch of tests, made me breathe into a machine after I'd been running on a treadmill. He told my mother I have severe asthma. Brady said I have to*

*limit my physical activity and keep an inhaler around for times when I wheeze and run into trouble. No big deal, he said, just something I have to live with. No big deal for him because he's not living with it! I'm not telling anybody, they'll only give me grief.'*

After this, Andrew writes a bunch of stuff about Darwin's research on the fascinating annelids. I close up the notebook, leaning back against the wall. The pigeons in their compartments keep up a constant cooing while one of them bobs her head up and down rhythmically. Maybe she's laying an egg and I shouldn't be staring at her at such an intimate moment. I'm looking at her but thinking about Andrew.

Why didn't Andrew tell me, his best friend, about the asthma? It bothers me until I remember what a complete jerk I've been recently. He can't know I've read this, he'd be totally pissed and never trust me again. I stand and slip it back into the hiding place. Before leaving I return to the club and sprinkle some water over the top of the worm farm.

Andrew's asthma is just one more negative, one more strike against him. On TV a commercial warns that asthma can kill you. Every time Taylor sees it he clutches his sides, panting, saying he's having an attack and is fighting for breath. I've never paid much attention to it before now.

It isn't until I start down the stairs that I remember my haircut.

"Shoot!" I yell and race out the barn door. The sun is already sinking low on the horizon and the sky is streaked with crazy shades of pink and purple. It must be well past three. It must be close to five. When I reach my yard, I'm breathing hard. My father is leaning up against the side of the car with his arms crossed, smoke practically pouring out of his ears.

# Chapter Ten

Sunday morning I'm in the kitchen getting myself a bowl of cereal when Strat knocks on the back door. I let him in and he sweeps past, almost suffocating me with a wave of perfume, or men's cologne. Maybe it is some kind of macho deodorant or something. Whatever it is, it's bad. I close the door and hold my arm against my nose.

Strat's wearing a dark green felt cowboy hat with a feather sticking out of the band. He takes it off, lays it gently on the counter, and starts smoothing his hair down. We hear Connie on the phone in the living room. Every time she either laughs or raises her voice, which is every couple of minutes, Strat's eyebrows shoot upwards. They're getting a major workout this morning.

"You here for a date?" I mumble, keeping my arm where it is. "You smell like dead animal."

"Lower your voice, phlegm wad," Strat hisses. "Where's your brother?"

He fixes his eyes on the glass cabinet behind me, using it as a mirror while he does battle with his hair. Connie laughs again and Strat's efforts grow frantic. I step aside so he gets a better view. There are a few choice pimples sprinkled across his chin with a film of white stuff smeared on them. In the middle of it all his beard is starting to grow, and the stiff dark hairs look like they're battling the pimples for space. The guy is a mess.

"Sleeping," I answer.

I can tell by his expression he thinks I'm lying.

"Wake him."

"What for?"

Strat stops preening and glares at me with steely eyes.

"Okay, okay," I say, holding my hands up and backing away.

I head for the stairs and Taylor's room. Connie is off the phone. She goes into the kitchen and I hear her ask, 'Man, what stinks in here?'

Taylor's room is silent as I knock on his door. I open it a crack. A wave of warm air smelling like dirty socks greets me. The room is almost completely dark except for a narrow shaft of sunlight coming in through the curtains, which are closed.

"Your boyfriend's here," I call out, "and he's not happy you're up here sleeping."

The lumpy form in the bed doesn't move but a low moan erupts from the room as I take the stairs, two at a time. Back in the kitchen, Connie is reading a magazine and drinking juice at the table and Strat is leaning, legs crossed and arms folded, against the counter. His hat is tilted down low over his eyes. Neither of them seems to be paying any attention to the other. Things seem to be going pretty well for old Strat.

I pour myself some juice and sit down across from Connie.

"Yo, Wills," she says, looking up.

"How'd you make out with the hurl babies?" I ask.

"Fine, came home clean this time."

I hold my hand across my mouth and make gagging noises. Connie smiles and goes back to her reading. Strat's personal scent is giving me a headache. He continues to lean against the counter with his eyes half closed, lizard style. He's either asleep, or thinking, it's tough to tell.

Taylor stumbles into the room, pulling a sweatshirt down over his head. His hair sticks out all over his head. It looks as if a family of bats spent the night there.

Strat grunts some greeting which Taylor returns. Nobody says anything until Taylor has wolfed down two glasses of milk, a banana, and some cereal. He leaves a few soggy rings floating in the milk.

"Today's the day," Strat finally drawls, looking meaningfully at Taylor. "It's warm out, bro, lose the sweatshirt."

"Cool," Taylor says.

He rises and puts his dishes into the sink. "What do I need to bring?"

Strat straightens up and hooks his thumbs into his pockets.

"Shovels, axes, pitchforks, weapons for doing serious damage," he drawls. He glances over at my sister to see if she's intrigued by his answer, but Connie is busy fixing the hoop in her left ear and pays no attention.

"We've got a massive job ahead of us," Strat tries again, "and it ain't gonna be easy."

Connie keeps her eyes on the magazine. Strat shoots her another quick look, adjusts the hat lower over his eyes and coughs a little. This is getting painful.

"So, okay, what are we fooling around here for? Let's get going," I say, because really, I can't stand it any longer.

I push my chair back from the table and head outside. Taylor springs up and rushes me, squeezing past and ramming me against the doorknob. He reaches the garage first and grabs our only shovel. I take the pitchfork. Strat emerges slowly from the back door. He removes his hat, smoothes his hair, and replaces it, sliding it into place at a jaunty angle over his eyes. It's warm and sunny and the birds are making a huge racket in the trees. Two robins flutter around in the grass. One of them keeps hopping all over the other one, which squawks, beats its wings, and tries to escape. It is hard to tell whether they're fighting, or mating. Strat looks at them, then back at the house. I swing my pitchfork at the bigger of the two birds and they fly away.

"Whatever," Taylor says. "Let's go."

He and Strat walk way ahead, ignoring me the entire way. When we get to Wyler's, everybody is outside the house waiting for Andrew. Adam's pushing a beat-up red wheelbarrow and the rest of them have shovels. As soon as Andrew appears we all head into the woods behind Barney's pasture. There are pine trees everywhere with big gobs of pitch running down their trunks and they smell great. Adam smears some of the sticky sap on one finger and chases Andrew and Pete around, trying to wipe it on their backs.

"Knock it off!" Strat growls. He's probably pretty ticked off he has to be here in the woods digging rather than back in our kitchen with my lovely sister. Abruptly he stops and jabs his shovel into the ground. "Right here. We'll dig here."

We stop while Andrew checks things out. Most of us have been playing in these woods since we could walk. But this is his turf, he knows them best.

"Uh uh, I don't think so. Not here. There's a stream right behind that fallen tree. If it rains hard, this ground turns into a little pond. It floods every spring," he says. "We'd be better off farther in on higher ground."

Adam and Colin nod their heads, but Pete just stares at Strat and blinks. He's afraid to cross him, even on the smallest level.

"What? You afraid of a little water?" Taylor asks. "Right here is good."

He steps forward and sticks his shovel beside Strat's. For a moment, nobody speaks. Adam picks up a pine cone and pitches it at a squirrel running along a branch high above us. The cone clips his tail as the squirrel springs up onto a higher limb.

Andrew shakes his head and stands up as straight as he can. He's got on tan work boots with thick rubber soles so he's a little taller than usual but alongside Strat he looks like a second grader. With a grunt, Strat digs deep, pulling up a shovel full of dirt and rocks. He's about to toss them off to one side when Andrew yells out.

"Hold on!"

Strat pauses, his shovel suspended in mid-air.

"Have you guys ever seen an earthworm that has been caught in a puddle? You know how it gets all bloated and distended, and, like, dead?"

A bunch of us nod, and even Taylor looks as if he is paying attention. Strat hurls the stuff on his shovel to one side.

"What's your point, Wyler?"

"Think about our tunnel. We're the mighty Annelids. Are we stupid enough to dig a tunnel in a place that could easily get flooded? In a week or so this whole area could be under several inches of water, maybe deeper. Do we want to risk that? After all, we're a heck of a lot smarter than worms, we can avoid sharing their fate when the rains come."

I don't know what the others are thinking, but I picture our soggy, bloated bodies floating at the tunnel's entrance, Strat's prized red lizard boots lying sideways in the water.

"No way, not me!" I say.

I head over to where Andrew pointed, with some of the others following. Taylor watches Strat as he throws his shovel down, crosses to the log, and peers over. The stream's there, a pretty decent flow of water trickling through the woods just as Andrew said. Taylor joins Strat, both of them peering down at the stream in silence. Then Strat removes his hat and scratches his head.

"It doesn't look like much now but it gets pretty massive after a storm," Andrew says. "Our tunnel would flood in no time. Worms can live for some time under water, people can't."

Between the bloated worms and swollen stream threats, Strat caves. He grunts, puts his hat back on his head, picks up his shovel and follows the rest of us. Taylor scurries along behind him. A couple of minutes later, Andrew stops.

"Here," he says. "Perfect. Pete, the plans please."

Pete produces his beautiful drawing, smoothing it out on the ground before weighing each corner down with a rock. This takes everybody by surprise and they huddle around in admiration.

Colin lets out a low whistle.

"Man. Think we can really dig that beauty?"

"Absolutely, piece of cake," Andrew says.

"We need to mark a spot for the entrance, then pace out the dimensions according to my scale," Pete says. "The ground is higher here, and pretty level, so this should work.

Strat scratches behind one ear.

"Huh?"

The feather in his hat ripples slightly in the breeze. It's a pivotal moment. Pete and Andrew are in charge, with Taylor and Strat following their lead.

"Scale?" Taylor mumbles. "What are you talking about?"

He and Strat look at each other.

"Sure, one inch equals a foot," Pete explains patiently, as if talking to a couple of toddlers. "Any good building plan needs a scale. The walls have to be a certain height and the tunnel a certain depth to support the ceiling we'll eventually construct, especially if we're putting a decent sized room at the end. We don't want to get the thing dug and finished and then have the roof cave in the first time somebody steps on it. We'd be buried alive."

Pete gives a little laugh, looking around to see if he's taken seriously.

Strat nods. Taylor doesn't know it but his mouth is hanging open, making him look even dumber than he is.

"Sure, I get it," Strat says. He tries to make it seem as if he is making the decisions which is kind of pathetic because we all know he isn't. "The roof has to be strong, strong enough for us to walk on. I knew that. So enough talk, let's get going already. Start digging."

Pete and Andrew pace out the exact dimensions for the tunnel as Adam, Colin and I find some rocks and sticks to mark them with. Mapped out the way we've done it makes the thing look like a board game. Everyone smart enough to remember gloves pulls them on as we each pick up something to dig with.

It's a relief to finally be here and start digging. Strat and Taylor begin most of the heavy ground breaking, working within the line of sticks, grunting and heaving and hitting rocks as they dig. I try but I don't get far. My pitchfork strikes a huge rock, sending a tingling sensation up my arm that kills. It is all I can do not to cry out.

"What's with all the rocks?" I ask, struggling to cut through the network of roots that block my shovel. Colin brings me a large pair of clippers and we work together cutting through the worst of them.

"Out of the way, runts," Taylor orders.

I'm more than happy to move over and let him work on enlarging this impossible hole so I help Pete move the dirt and debris in the wheelbarrow. We learn to fill it just half way, because even then it's amazingly heavy.

"Let's dump it here," Pete says, motioning to a spot near where the end of the tunnel will be. "We can use it to cover the top when we're finished digging."

"How will the roof be able to support the weight of the soil?" I ask. I'm glad Pete is in charge of the plans and not me.

"That's why the angle of the walls is so important," Pete says, pushing his glasses back on his nose. "If my calculations are correct, it'll be sufficiently strong and should hold up. We should be fine."

Andrew and Colin struggle to remove the biggest rocks from the dirt pile so it can be used to cover the plywood when the tunnel's finished. They hurl them off to the side, and for a while, all we hear is grunting and the ringing of rocks as they hit the pile and either bust apart or roll off. Some of the roots we've cut through are as thick as my wrist.

They get tossed onto the pile too.

For a couple of hours we work, taking turns dumping the wheelbarrow and moving rocks. By the time we stop for a lunch break I'm so exhausted I'm not sure how I'll even lift a shovel again, much less dig. A small but dedicated swarm of annoying gnats has been steadily flying around our heads. Andrew uses his bandana to remove one from the corner of Adam's eye. He's been coughing a lot, so I tell him to take a break. He looks tired, his face flushed from the effort of moving earth.

"Quit telling me to take it easy," he complains between coughing fits. "Stop acting like my mom."

Adam throws his shovel down and collapses on the ground next to Andrew.

"Yeah, Wills, lay off."

Andrew sticks his tongue out at me.

"I wouldn't do that," I warn. "You'll wind up eating a bug sandwich."

"Speaking of sandwiches, I'll go home and make some lunch," Andrew says.

His jeans are plastered with dirt and when he takes his work gloves off, his hands are already starting to show angry red blisters.

"Nasty," Taylor says. "It looks like we've been digging graves or something."

Adam lies flat on his back and stares up at the trees. The tops of the pines are swaying because there's a good breeze. It makes a soft whooshing sound as it passes through them.

Strat leans on his shovel. Beads of sweat dot his upper lip.

"Shapiro, you dead or alive?"

Adam shuts his eyes and crosses his arms over his face.

"Dead," he moans.

Strat laughs.

"What a bunch of wimps!" he crows. "We've only gotten started on this thing. This is day one. You mutts will never make it through initiation, trust me."

My arms are sore and my back is killing me from all the lifting. We've been digging all morning and the tunnel isn't even very deep. It's just a jagged, gaping hole in the ground, a huge dark snake. I suddenly remember that Andrew told me that early men called worms serpents. It seems like a big name for an insignificant creature, but maybe they were on to something. I mean, that Darwin guy Andrew goes on about said worms were powerful creatures in their own way. Moving earth is not as easy as you'd think.

"Hey, how about a code name for this thing? We need to be able to talk about it without anyone else knowing," I suggest. "What about 'serpent'?"

"Good idea," Adam says. "I'm not so sure my parents would be happy knowing what we're doing. They'd probably sign me up for a summer baseball league or something."

"Mine too," Pete says. "Computer camp."

So I tell everybody what Andrew uncovered in his research and we agree that we'll use serpent to identify the tunnel when we don't want anyone to know what we're up to. Andrew is pleased I gave him credit and asks me to go back with him to help with the food.

"Hurry up," Taylor orders. "I'm starving."

Casually I kick some dirt in his direction, trying to make it look like an accident, and it sprays across his legs. Before he can get to his feet I'm off and running, with Andrew close behind. We're both laughing so hard I get a pain in my side. It feels great to move, to get away from Strat and my bully brother. Out into the sunshine and away from the cool, dark woods.

# Chapter Eleven

We're still laughing as we reach Barney's pasture. The sun is slanting through the thinning pines and it's a lot warmer in the open field. Some birds are busy pecking a fresh pile of Barney's manure, hunting for bits of undigested grain. Andrew seems to be struggling for breath so I slow to a walk.

"Hey, you okay?"

I rest my hand on his back. He's breathing pretty hard and doesn't answer. It really stinks knowing about his asthma without him knowing--we usually don't keep many things from each other. But I can't tell him I've read his journal. That's invasion of privacy or something.

"Yeah," he says weakly, "don't tell my mother I've been coughing or she'll make me wear a hat and scarf."

"In June? That's crazy. Tell her it's seventy degrees out. Feels like it."

Mrs. Wyler is overprotective, but Andrew is her only child. The sun is so bright it's making the buds on the trees practically burst open in front of our eyes.

"You tell her, she'll never believe me."

Mrs. Wyler is in the kitchen, just taking brownies out of the oven. Andrew and I make chicken sandwiches, pack some fruit, and add half the tray of brownies to the old canvas book bag his mother gives us. She's made a huge Thermos of lemonade and tells Andrew to add some ice.

"Strat wanted Gatorade," Andrew mumbles.

Mrs. Wyler wipes off the outside of the Thermos before handing it to me.

"Strat Sherwood is part of this? I thought you've had trouble with him."

"Nah," Andrew says. "He's all talk. We let him think he's part of the plan, but we're just letting him in so we have someone to take care of the grunt work. Besides, he and Taylor are buddies."

"What grunt work?" Mrs. Wyler asks.

Andrew acts as if he hasn't heard her. He stuffs all the food into the bag and gives his mother a hug.

"Are you okay, taking it easy?" she asks.

She reaches over and touches his hair. Even if I didn't already know what I do about Andrew's asthma I'd wonder what she meant.

"Ma!" Andrew says, knocking her hand away. "Lay off! If anything I'm being smothered by an overprotective mother."

He pulls his sweatshirt over his head and throws it on a chair.

"Thanks a lot, Mrs. Wyler," I say. "This looks great."

As soon as the back door slams shut behind us, Andrew starts in on me.

"Talk about a kiss-up!" he complains. "Thanks Mrs. Wyler, this looks super!" When he crosses his eyes and smiles sweetly I punch him on the shoulder.

Going up through the woods we hear the guys well before we see them. If we want to keep the entire neighborhood from discovering us, we're going to have to tell them to keep quiet. After we reach the serpent they fall upon us, grabbing at the food.

"Hey!" Andrew yells, spinning away from them. "Down boys!"

He opens the bag and hands out the sandwiches.

"What are you, the friggin' den mother?" Taylor asks. He shoves most of his sandwich into his mouth, leaving his cheeks bulging. "No chips?"

I look at him in disgust.

"Tell you what, Taylor, you take care of the next meal."

He stops chewing and opens his mouth wide, showing me the mess inside and spilling some of it down his shirt. A couple of the guys laugh, then we finish up and get back to the tunnel construction with a little less energy than we started out with.

Andrew and Pete collect worms from the dirt on our shovels and put them in a paper cup. We've decided they're sacred animals who have earned our protection. Every heaping mound we lift out of the earth is rich and spilling over as they twist and turn against the light.

For most of the rest of the afternoon we dig and haul roots and rocks until we're all exhausted. We agree to meet after school every day for the rest of the week. Thursday's a half day, after that, school's out for summer.

"Friday it is," Strat says darkly. "It's time to stop fooling around."

I lower my shovel for a second and wipe both hands on my pants.

"Why Friday?" I ask.

"The tunnel will be mostly done by then. The party's over. Time to start initiation."

Pete steps up alongside me and leans on his shovel.

"I forget," he says, "what exactly do we have to do?"

Some dirt is smudged across Pete's cheek and his jeans are filthy. Taylor narrows his eyes and licks his lips. He's beginning to resemble a snake, in more ways than one. If he starts eating insects the transformation will be complete.

"You know, we crawl on our bellies, one by one, the entire length of the tunnel till we reach the room at the end," he tells Pete. "It was your buddy Will's idea, remember?"

He reaches over and lifts Pete's glasses off his face. "Don't think you'll be needing these, my friend. They might get dirty, or break."

Last year Pete failed the eye exam in school even with glasses on. He had to get new, stronger ones with thicker lenses. I guess he's pretty blind without them.

Pete grabs the glasses out of Taylor's hands and the frames kind of twist and bend. Taylor and Strat laugh. I dig a tissue out of my back pocket and hand it to Pete so he can wipe them off.

He looks different without the glasses, his eyes tiny, his face full and pale.

"Thanks," he mumbles.

I think we've all had enough for one day.

"How about we finish up and meet again tomorrow?" I ask. "We'll have to keep working on this all week and see how it goes."

"The job will get done," Strat says, "if you kids don't crap out on us." He looks at Taylor and nods.

"Yeah, I gotta go," Colin says. "It's late."

The light in the woods is getting thin which means dusk is approaching. None of us has a watch and Taylor's cell isn't charged so it is tough to tell the time. Andrew and I start picking up the garbage from lunch and putting it in the bag. We empty the last heavy load of dirt from the wheelbarrow. Only then do we realize that Strat and Taylor have vanished, leaving their shovels lying on the ground. Colin picks them up and brings them over.

"You can't leave these, Wills. If it rains they'll be ruined."

"My dad will be ripped if that happens," I say.

Thanks to my brother I have to lug everything all the way home, solo. We agree on a time for Tuesday and start back. At the edge of the pasture Adam and Colin head off towards Adam's house, pushing the wheelbarrow.

"Later," Colin yells.

"Three-thirty," Andrew answers.

Together we carry the extra shovels all the way back to the shed. Andrew's mother has turned on the porch light. It throws a warm circle of yellow illuminating the steps. He puts the bag down, leaning his stuff against the stair railing.

"Hey, you never finished telling me, how come you know all this stuff about Darwin?" I suddenly remember to ask. "And why did he waste time studying worms? Couldn't he have found something more interesting?"

Andrew shakes his head.

"You never heard of Charles Darwin?" he asks. "Man, I can't believe that."

I hate when he does this, treats me like some kind of moron just because I'm not as smart. Before he can answer, Mrs. Wyler opens the porch door.

"Dinner's on," she tells Andrew. "Wills, we're having steak. You're invited if you'd like to join us."

"Oh, thanks," I say. "But I've got to get home." No way my parents would let me stay on a school night, even if it is the end of the year.

Andrew smiles and follows his mother up the stairs, turning for a split second at the top before he goes in.

"For your information, Wills, he didn't only study worms. He studied tons of things; plants, fossils, even pigeons. Worms were just part of it. He believed the diversity of species made us strong. It's kind of true for people, too. See you."

I raise my hand, then turn to pick up the shovels. It's pretty hard carrying my stuff along with Taylor and Strat's, but who else is going to do it? Alone in the dark I concentrate on getting it all home without dropping stuff or falling. And even though I know the path by heart, I listen for the slightest sound or movement in the woods. It would be just like Taylor to leap out at me from the shadows, just to see if he can scare the pants off his little brother.

# Chapter Twelve

On Tuesday, the sun is so fierce and hot that almost everybody shows up at school in tee shirts and shorts. Mr. Duff, our math teacher, has difficulty getting us to convert fractions into decimals so he starts writing names on the board. The first one to get a check beside their name misses recess. It's like the worst thing he could threaten, so everybody calms down and tries to focus.

Through the open windows I see a bunch of girls and their coach outside playing field hockey. Some of them have huge, muscular thighs that bulge impressively as they race up and down the field, hacking the heck out of each others' legs. When the bell finally rings, we burst through the doors and out onto the grass.

"Yo, George!" I call to the best kickball player in our grade, "let's pick teams."

We call George Demetros "the Greek." He's already 5'9" and an awesome athlete. He and I form a team and start choosing. We have only about a half hour outside so I don't waste any time. When I pick Andrew, a voice in back of me hisses 'bad move' in my ear. I ignore it. Andrew may not be great at sports but he is my best friend.

"C'mon! Let's play!" someone yells. As the faded red ball flies over the ground, the basketball court, where we play, is transformed into a mass of running, leaping bodies. Right away we get the other team out, then we're up. George kicks first. Everybody's screaming and yelling as he sends the ball all the way out towards the soccer field and then races around the bases, arms tucked into his sides and head high.

"Way to go, Greek!" I yell, slapping his raised hand as he comes in.

George is grinning, with sweat forming small beads of lace on his forehead until he wipes it off with the bottom of his shirt.

By now recess is almost over, the score is tied and the other team is up. Someone kicks a hard ball that rockets past Andrew. He dives, misses, then scrambles to his feet and starts after it. Everybody is screaming and hollering and I wish it was anybody but Andrew in pursuit.

Suddenly the bell rings and everybody turns back toward the building. Andrew, still running, is only half way across the field.

"Andrew! The bell! Don't kill yourself!" I cup my hands and yell, but I can't tell if he even hears me.

He sort of collapses on the ball and rolls with it for a few feet. It's hard to know whether he falls or throws himself on it. When I reach him, he is coughing and breathing hard, his face sideways in the grass. I sink down and put my hand in the middle of his back, which heaves as he fights to catch his breath. I'm pretty freaked out and I'm breathing hard, too.

"You okay, buddy? Andrew?"

It takes a minute before he turns over and sits up, and when he does he looks awful. His face is flushed and he's fighting for air. The wheezing noise he is making is really weird; I've never heard anything like it before. I have about a split second to decide whether to just lift him up or try to get some serious help. Then I realize it's faster just to bring him in myself.

"C'mon," I grunt as I reach under and sort of haul him up by the armpits. For a little guy he sure is heavy. "I'm taking you to the nurse. Leave the ball."

By the time I half drag, half carry him into the nurse's office he's struggling to breathe. He hasn't said a word since I lifted him off the ground, and really, I'm not sure he can. As usual, Mrs. Brotherton's tiny office is packed with the weak and the wounded. Some kid is stretched out on her green vinyl couch with an ice pack across his forehead. I start to explain about Andrew but Brotherton cuts me off with a wave of her hand.

"Thanks for bringing him in, I'll take it from here," she says curtly.

She leads Andrew over to a bench, sits him down, hands me a hall pass and then pushes me gently to the door. Some rescue, I think as it clicks closed in my face.

"Is that any way to treat a hero?" I ask.

A girl sidling down the hallway watches me nervously and presses against the opposite wall as she passes. She looks as if she thinks I may actually bite her or something. I bark at her, twice, just so she'll have something to tell her friends. Then I leave, taking the long way back to Spanish class where I've already missed the first fifteen minutes.

Not long after I get to class the dismissal bell rings. On the bus I see that Andrew's missing. I nod to Mr. Shepley and slide into a seat in front of B.J. and his merry band. B.J.'s got a bag of peanuts and he is busy shooting them at kids when he thinks Shepley isn't looking. The bus pulls out and away from the curb, crawling along behind a line of other buses waiting to exit. A peanut hits the side of my face and bounces off onto the floor. No big deal, but enough to make me lose it. All year B.J. has tormented the kids on this bus and all year we've tried to avoid him. Mr. Shepley's job is to keep order, but it is impossible for him to do that and drive at the same time. I think of Connie, of what she would do, before I spring into action.

Leaning over as far as I can without actually falling, I bash old B.J. over the head with my math book, hard. The book makes a satisfying thud when it hits, which I take a second to appreciate. Quickly, before B.J. has time to react, I grab my stuff and slide into the seat directly behind Mr. Shepley. Nobody ever sits behind Shepley, it's an unwritten rule.

Old B.J. starts howling and clutches his head. Then, before he and his nasty gang can retaliate, a funny thing happens. It takes a split second before I recognize the sound of applause. It swells up from the back of the bus and ripples forward. Jumping to my feet, I move quickly out into the aisle and bow deeply, swaying from side to side with the motion of the bus. Some of the younger kids give me a standing ovation.

B.J. is so shocked he keeps moaning and rests his head against the back of the seat with his eyes closed. There's no blood gushing or anything so we know he's not mortally wounded. He's just going for an Oscar nomination, playing to the balcony as my mom would say. I glance up and catch Mr. Shepley looking at me in the rearview mirror. He winks, I smile. By the time I hop off at my stop I'm feeling kinda like a hero.

# Chapter Thirteen

As soon as I'm home I call Andrew.

"He's had kind of a rough day and he's resting, Wills," Mrs. Wyler whispers. "I'll have him call you when he wakes."

Before I can fill her in about what happened on the playground, she hangs up. Over a snack I tell my mother everything, about the kickball game and Andrew. From her reaction I'm pretty sure Mrs. Wyler has already filled her in about Andrew's asthma. But she goes along with the party line and reveals nothing.

"Pretty weird, huh? I mean, what would make Andrew collapse like that?"

"It must have been scary, Wills. I really don't know. A lot of things could make you faint. Maybe he was dehydrated, that happens in the warm weather, or maybe just overtired."

I look my mother right in the eye. I know, and she knows, that this wasn't the case. I shake my head.

"He didn't faint, Ma. He couldn't breathe, that's different. He was making these weird noises, like gasping or something, trying to catch his breath. It sounded as if there was something rattling around in his chest. Besides, Andrew has never fainted in his life."

"Well, whatever it was Wills, I'm glad you were able to get him help," she says, and leaves it at that.

I don't tell my mother about B.J. She'd tell my father, and he'd give me a hard time.

They always tell us to stay out of fights, to turn and walk away, as if it's that simple.

Sometimes you just get pushed to the wall and have to do something, that's all. Maybe now B.J. will think twice before he tortures anyone again. Or maybe he'll come after me, who knows?

I bend an arm and flex, wondering if Strat would let me use his basement gym to pump iron. I could use some extra brawn. I'm still examining my muscles when Taylor emerges from his room on a homework break and leans into the refrigerator.

"Any good grunts?" he asks.

My mother stands, pulls a bag of bagels out of a drawer and tosses it at him.

"Don't hang on the door, Taylor," she says with a sigh. "Get the cream cheese out then close the fridge. Is your homework finished?"

Next year Taylor will be in high school, and schoolwork is pretty far down on his list. He's supposed to do it as soon as he gets home. Now he looks across the kitchen at her with a wounded expression.

"Ma, whaddya think?" he says. Then he looks my way. "Hey dork. I hear you caused some major trouble on the bus today. A real riot. Nice going."

He takes the end of the knife and scrapes the cream cheese off with his teeth.

"Taylor!" my mother says.

"I hear B.J. is after your skinny butt," he continues, pointing the knife at me.

"Taylor!"

My mother hates this kind of language. She should hear the way kids talk, this is nothing. I look evenly at my brother. We both know he's trying to get me grounded.

"B.J. was being a pain in the neck, harassing little kids," I tell my mother.

Just then, the phone rings and I leap up and grab it.

"Hello?"

"Yo, Wills," Andrew says. He sounds good, like his old self. "My mother said you called to check on me. Relax, dude, I'm fine."

I take the phone and move into the living room.

"Yeah? You could have fooled me. It sounded as if you were in big trouble. You were crumpled on the ground and could hardly breathe. It was crazy."

For a minute there's no response.

"I know," he finally says. "I sounded worse than I was. I think I must have knocked the wind out of myself when I fell or something."

"Yeah, well, don't do it again, okay?"

I'm letting him down easy, but if he can't bring himself to tell me the truth I can't force it.

"You missed my victory on the bus this afternoon. Harris and his band started in with their usual nonsense, and something snapped. I lost it, just couldn't take it anymore. It was amazing. I finally put that scum out of commission!"

Andrew laughs lightly. He's probably glad we're back on safe ground.

"No way!"

I look toward the kitchen. My mom is still talking to Taylor so I lower my voice and cup my hand around the receiver.

"You should have seen it. He was shooting peanuts at everybody, you know, pulling his usual stuff and harassing kids. One hit me in the face so I lost it. I took my math book and clobbered him over the head. I mean, I nailed him!"

Andrew gasps and whoops with joy. I can tell I've made his day. It hasn't been a great one but so what, I've made it anyway.

"Yo, Superman!" he says, and we crack up. "Now he's going to be after you though, Wills. That won't be funny."

"No worries, mate," I say. I heard this on a show about Australia. That's how they talk, they call each other mate. "School is out Thursday. I think I took care of any brains he had left. He isn't going to mess with me for a while. You feeling up to a visit to the serpent this afternoon? Everybody's going to be there."

"My mother won't let me," Andrew says sadly. "She's making me take it easy."

"Raw deal. But you should probably save your strength for Friday anyway. You'll need it. Read some Darwin, do some worm research, get some rest. I'll call tomorrow and tell you how everything goes."

"Peace," Andrew says, and we hang up.

Back in the kitchen my mother tells me that Strat and Taylor went over to Wyler's and said to meet them there. I can tell she's happy we're all hanging out together. Taylor and I haven't done anything like this in years. She wants to believe we're doing something wholesome, like practicing tying Boy Scout knots or something.

I give her a hug and head over to the woods. Colin and Adam are already there digging and Pete arrives a couple of minutes later. There's a big mound of dirt beside the tunnel so I can see Taylor and Strat have been working hard. The thing is not only long it's fairly deep, too. The ends of roots broken by the shovels are protruding from the sides, looking like long brown arms reaching out of the ground, and most of the bigger rocks have been pulled out. Strat is standing in what will be the chamber, a room so deep it reaches just under his shoulders. He's sweating so hard there's a dark half circle under each of his arm pits. If he's wearing cologne today it isn't going to help.

"Where've you been, butthead? Get busy," Taylor says and throws a shovel at me. "No more breaks until we're finished."

For more than four hours we grunt and dig and haul loads of dirt away, making the tunnel deeper and smoothing out the walls. Strat and Taylor pry the remaining rocks loose, using a pickaxe to release them from the packed earth. Pete, Colin, Adam and I lift them into the wheelbarrow for dumping farther up in the woods. The sounds of metal against stone ring out from time to time as the tunnel gets deeper. I don't think any of us realized how hard digging this tunnel was going to be or how much teamwork would be involved. Even though I hated to include Taylor and Strat, there's no way we could have done it without them.

Adam is the first one to give way to exhaustion. He throws his shovel down, stops working and stretches out in the middle of the tunnel.

"Man, I need a break," he says. "My arms are killing me. I don't think I can move one more load of dirt. I'm wasted."

"Stop whining, Shapiro," Strat orders. "If I'd known I was going to be doing this thing with a bunch of babies I wouldn't have signed on. Crawl forward to see how you fit."

Adam flips over and inches forward, army style, keeping his head low. When he reaches the end we let out a yell. This whole thing really might work and now I can't imagine why I'd doubted it in the first place.

"Yo! Are we going to be able to see in there after we close it in with the roof?" Colin asks. "It'll be totally dark."

"Andrew suggested candles," I say.

Actually, Andrew dreamt we put candles in to light the way, but I didn't want to share that. Something tells me these guys wouldn't appreciate the dream machine. Strat scratches under one arm, ape style, and scowls.

"Why candles, who says we need light?" he asks. "And where is that little runt Wyler anyway?"

"Sick. He'll be here tomorrow."

It's growing dark, close to dinnertime. We decide to meet again tomorrow and work on finishing the sides and roof. The roof is going to be tricky, the most challenging part of this whole tunnel construction. Adam offers to bring the plywood his father said we could use.

"Better show Pete to make sure what you have will be wide enough to cover the top," I tell him. "This thing is way bigger than I thought it would be."

"Yeah, it's a lot wider than I thought," Adam says. "I'll bring extra sheets so we'll have enough. Want to help, Pete?"

The two of them leave to go check out the plywood at Adam's house. The others pick up their sweatshirts and shovels and they take off, too. I hang around for a while, just because I

71

want to take the time to look at what we've done. Lowering myself into the tunnel, I stretch out on my back, just to see what it feels like. The birds are making a huge racket and when I look up I see some black crows chasing a bigger bird. It's probably a hawk or maybe even an owl, they usually gang up on birds of prey that threaten their turf.

The earth I'm lying on is damp and cool even though it's been a hot day. It smells good, too, reminding me how much I love being outside in these woods. I close my eyes and listen to the cawing of the crows, thinking about worms, Andrew, this summer and our club. When I open them an earthworm is wriggling out of the wall by my left arm. His brownish-pink head pushes and pokes as he fights his way through the soil.

"Annelid, buddy, you look ridiculous," I say. "How's it going?"

It's silly lying in the tunnel talking to a worm. Andrew would definitely approve. Seeing this slimy guy appear right now must be some sort of sign. Andrew would consider it an omen, a signal that our club has some higher purpose on earth. I'm not into that stuff, though. A worm is just a worm. You've seen one, you've seen them all. But still, all this work on the tunnel has given me a new appreciation for these earth movers. I wouldn't tell Andrew that but it's true. Gently I pull this one out of the dirt, careful not to break him in two as he turns and twists wildly against my touch. Then I place him on the tunnel floor.

"Better be out of here by dawn if you don't want to be some bird's breakfast."

Jumping up I climb out of the hole and brush all the dirt and leaves off my clothes. Before leaving I look back, once. The tunnel looks crude, like some menacing black gash in the otherwise tranquil woods. It doesn't really fit in with the whole peaceful scene. It looks, instead, like something evil, something vaguely threatening. All the good vibes I had earlier, when we were feeling as if our project might actually work, have disappeared. I shiver a little to think the whole ugly project was my idea.

Standing there I wonder about initiation and crawling through the tunnel in the dark. You never really know how you're going to react to something like that until it's too late. I hope I won't be scared to be closed into a tight, narrow, black space, with no room to move, because some people are. Claustrophobics, they're called. I hope I'm not one of them.

It's nearly dark as I start home. Half way down the trail I see bushes moving and hear something rustling up ahead. Strat and Taylor, waiting to ambush? I move forward slowly, careful not to step on twigs or break any branches. My heart is pounding so hard I'm positive it will give me away. Near the spot the noise came from I leap forward, waving my arms, and pounce into the bushes.

"Yaaaa!" I yell, hoping to scare them. Hoping to get them before they get me. Instead there's a huge whirring noise as a bunch of wild turkeys fly straight at me, clumsy as they work to lift their heavy bodies into the air. If possible, they look even more startled and frightened than I am. All I can think to do is hit the ground, fast, as the squawking things barely rise above my flattened body and disappear into the darkening trees.

# Chapter Fourteen

"What we need is a lottery," Taylor declares the next day, "that's a fair way of determining who'll be the first victim--I mean, who'll go first on Friday."

"Ha, ha, very funny," I say.

Andrew's eyes are open so wide he looks as if he's just seen a ghost. He managed to make it to school today but still looks wiped out.

"What do you mean?" he asks Taylor. "What kind of lottery?"

We're meeting at the club to discuss a few things before we go out to finish digging and put the roof on the serpent. Right now we're trying to figure out how to handle the Annelid initiation. Taylor and Strat are struggling to control things and neither of them is in a pretty mood. They didn't laugh at any of my worm jokes, not even the one that got Colin rolling around on the floor howling in delight.

"Don't play dumb, Wyler," Strat says in disgust. "You know how a lottery works. We pick numbers out of my hat, and then we'll run through initiation in order, starting from the lowest number to the highest. Highest goes last."

I look over at Andrew. He just shrugs.

"I guess that's okay," Andrew says. "Seems fair."

Nobody wants to go first, nobody wants to take the trial run. Pete raises his hand just above his head as if somebody is going to shoot it off if he goes any higher. Taylor, of course, ignores him.

"Got any paper?" he asks Andrew.

Strat removes his hat, strokes the feather once, and hands it over. Most of his hair is smooshed down, except for one patch in front which kind of sticks straight up like a crest. He reminds me of a giant cockatiel, only his eyes are too mean. Not even his old buddy Taylor has the guts to inform him that he looks like a fool. We move on with the meeting with him looking completely ridiculous. The more I try to avoid looking, the more I can't keep my eyes off him. Everybody else seems to be having the same problem. I glance over at Adam, pressing my hand against my mouth so I won't burst out laughing.

"What's so funny, idiot?" Strat snarls. "You got something you want to share?"

"Nothing," I say, "not a thing." I bite my lip, concentrating on my lap to avoid looking at him.

The room is quiet while Taylor rips a sheet of paper into seven small pieces, writing a number on each. He folds them in half and drops each into the green hat. The soft sound of pigeons cooing is the only noise in the barn so I figure Barney must be out in his pasture rolling around in the sweet smelling grass.

"Pete has a question," Adam says to no one in particular, although Pete's hand is still half raised so this is obvious to everybody. Strat takes his hat and shakes it, mixing the numbers. The papers bounce around inside like Mexican jumping beans.

"What?" I ask.

"I forget exactly what we'll be doing tomorrow," he says in a shaky voice. He's blinking rapidly and looks about ready to wet his pants. "Tell me again."

"Jeez," I say, throwing up my hands. "It's not that complicated, how many times do we have to go over this? You pick a number out of the hat, take your turn, crawl into the tunnel, through the passage, and wind up at the room at the end. Bingo. That's it. You're done. The walls will have a couple of candles along the sides so it won't be that dark."

Colin leans forward, his hands on his knees.

"Don't candles need oxygen to burn?" he asks. "What if they go out before everyone gets through?"

Strat sits back and cracks the knuckles on his left hand.

"That's why you don't want to be last," he says sweetly. "The sucker who's last could be doing his crawl in total darkness."

Andrew and I look at each other. It's something neither of us thought of.

"Can we all fit into that chamber?" Adam asks. "Is it big enough?"

"I don't know," I admit. "Ask Pete, he designed it."

"I think so. It'll be kind of tight, so we may have to curl up a little but we should fit."

"Sardines," Taylor says. "We'll make like sardines."

*I think about my dream, about being stuck in the plastic cocoon with Andrew and not being able to breathe.*

"Enough," I say. "Let's just do this and get it over with."

Taylor laughs, too loud, because he knows some of us are getting freaked out and he's loving it. Strat finishes shaking the hat, reaches out, and thrusts it towards Andrew.

"You first, shrimp."

Andrew lifts out the first piece of paper as if it were a stick of dynamite, and one by one we follow, holding on to them but not looking. They sit politely folded on our laps like napkins at a dinner party. Strat reaches for the last piece and puts his hat on the floor.

Slowly he unfolds the paper.

"Number seven," he says.

It turns out that Pete has the lowest number, so he'll go first. Then comes Adam, then Taylor, then me, then Colin, then Andrew. Strat's last, which positively thrills him. Is it possible he could have rigged this? For all we know, he'll let us go first then block up the entrance, trapping us inside. Andrew and I exchange looks.

"Any of you guys don't make it, I'm not coming in," Strat says darkly. "You'll be my guinea pigs. Canaries in the mines."

"Huh?" Taylor's confused. I must admit, I'm not sure what he's talking about either.

Andrew sinks back in his chair.

"They used to send canaries down into the coal mines to see if there was enough oxygen to keep a man alive," Andrew says, then leans forward. "I'm impressed you knew that, Strat."

"What, you think you're the only guy with brains?" Strat asks.

Just then there's a knock at the door and Connie pokes her head into the room. I guess we look pretty weird sitting in a circle on our little crates.

"Hi," Connie says. "Am I interrupting anything? Can I come in?"

"Sure, c'mon in." I jump up and close the door behind her.

Strat rises and pushes his crate back.

"Hey Connie," Andrew says. He goes over and she gives him a quick hug, which is not lost on Strat. All of a sudden he looks kind of miserable, like a guy stuck in the tunnel of love without enough air to breathe. He may be clueless, but he's totally staring at her.

"So this is the famous club," Connie smiles and looks around. "Very cool."

Andrew takes her arm and leads her over to the worm farm. She leans against him, listening as he goes through his worm routine. Our meeting starts to break up, and Taylor, Pete, Adam and Colin head out to work on the tunnel. I tell them we'll follow shortly.

"You'd better, shorty," Taylor cracks, and leaves. We hear him laughing as he clumps down the stairs.

Someday I'm going to write a book about what it's like to have a baboon for a brother.

It'll probably be a best seller, so many people will relate to it.

"Okay, so, why worms?" I hear Connie ask Andrew.

Strat is standing so close behind her she must feel his hot breath on her neck.

"Why not?" Andrew asks happily. "I did a science project and discovered what completely amazing creatures they are.

They do the earth a lot of good, they clean up the bad stuff as they produce fertilizer. In fact, they're the original environmentalists."

I let out a huge, exaggerated yawn and cover my mouth with my hand. Andrew shoots me a dirty look. Strat's still standing behind Connie, almost on top of her in fact, happy to be breathing in her natural perfume. Any closer and he'd knock her over.

All of a sudden, Andrew notices.

"Yo, Strat, you having a bad hair day or something?" he asks.

It's like waving a red flag at a bull. As Connie turns to look, Strat's hand shoots up, locates the unruly hair and frantically tries to smooth it down. This isn't easy without saliva, or water of some kind, but even Strat knows it wouldn't be cool to come up with something usable in front of a girl so he finally gives up and clamps his hat back on, looking as if he wants to seriously hurt someone. Moving sideways, he gets his face right up against Andrew's. For a split second I think that he might spit on, or maybe even bite, Andrew.

"You're dead meat, worm boy, better watch your back," he snarls, then turns and walks out, slamming the door behind him. Connie, Andrew and I look at each other.

Connie bursts out laughing.

"Worm boy? Is he for real? What a complete fool," she says, shaking her head.

With hands on my hips I turn to face Andrew.

"Are you crazy?"

Connie doesn't realize the stakes here. By making Strat look stupid in front of Connie Andrew humiliated him. And now he'll pay. I cross over to the window and look out. Strat has a shovel over one shoulder as he disappears into the woods. Connie stays a little longer, asks Andrew a few more questions about worms and leaves to go baby-sitting. As soon as the door closes behind her I sink down and put my head in my hands.

"Andrew," I moan. "He's going to kill you."

"What? He was practically on top of her! You saw it. I was just trying to get him to back off."

Andrew slides down next to me and I can tell from the set of his chin he's feeling stubborn. I realize then that I was right about Andrew. Strat isn't the only one with a crush on Connie. Is everyone I know in love with my sister? All of a sudden, I'm tired of the whole stinking mess. I'm not sure if I'm up to either the tunnel initiation or dealing with the guys swarming my sister.

"Go home and get some rest," I suggest. "I'll help the others finish up."

Andrew slams his hand down on the floor.

"Stop telling me what to do! You're driving me crazy, Wills, you really are. You're worse than my parents."

I close my eyes for a few seconds and take a deep breath.

"Okay, fine. Do what you want. Only stay away from Strat if you value your life. He's not going to forget what you just pulled. Let's get moving and get out there before they finish the whole thing without us."

Andrew stands and kind of half-heartedly kicks the nearest crate, which slides into the worm farm. It's so light the tank doesn't budge. We head downstairs and out the door. Mrs. Wyler is busy spreading manure over her garden, and Barney is lying in one corner of the pasture. He's on his side, with his big belly sticking up, not moving. Once in a while his black tail sweeps up and knocks the flies off. The sun is hot but once we enter the woods the temperature cools. Tomorrow might be altogether different, but this feels like the perfect day.

# Chapter Fifteen

We hear them working long before we see them. My brother's voice rises above the rest as he shouts orders. I'm hoping one day soon everybody will revolt, tie him up, and throw him into the chamber at the end of the tunnel for a little rest and relaxation. That would fix him.

"Well, well, look who's decided to join us," he says when we appear. "Little late, aren't you, girls?"

Most of the plywood is already in place, making a near perfect roof. Strat and Colin are busy shoveling dirt across the top, Pete and Adam are off gathering pine needles and leaves to spread over it for camouflage. Strat's concentrating so hard on his work he doesn't look up.

"What happened to your ear?" I ask Taylor. A small, gold hoop is dangling from his left lobe. He steps over a pile of dirt and wiggles it in my face.

"Pierced, little brother, that's what. Ever seen a pierced ear before? Don't tell the old man, he's not going to be happy."

"No way!"

"Yeah, what do you think he's gonna do about it, huh?" my brother asks, turning his back on me.

Adam comes over and touches my arm.

"He's full of it," he says, "it's just a cheap ring he found and stuck on. It isn't real."

I was pretty sure that even Taylor wouldn't have been stupid enough to pierce his ear, my father would have a fit. There'd be a real scene. No son of his would go around wearing an earring.

"It's fake!" Andrew whispers.

We bump fists, then grab rakes and start smoothing dirt over the boards. It's a lot easier than the digging and more rewarding. Pete and Colin scatter the leaves and pine needles they've gathered on top. Strat has placed the longest boards over the chamber, and by the time we finish raking it smooth the only way you can tell the tunnel exists is by the large hole at the entrance.

"What do we do about this?" Adam asks.

We look at each other.

"Pete?" I turn to him as he walks over to the hole and squats down.

"We'll need a rock, or a log, but it has to be big enough to pretty much hide this thing."

"Yeah, but we'll need to be able to move it back and forth, so not too big," I say.

None of us want to state the obvious. Taylor and Strat can't be the only ones able to move the thing. That would be insane.

Fortunately this goes right over my brother's head.

"Right," he says. "Now where we gonna find that?"

We fan out through the woods and start searching. Andrew sticks close, right by my side, like I'm some sort of bodyguard or something. Now that he has had time to think about it, he is probably pretty nervous that Strat will be seeking revenge after looking like an idiot in front of Connie. We both know that when Strat comes after Andrew, there won't be much I can do to protect him.

We search everywhere, over toward the edges of Barney's pasture and up the hill behind the pines. We find rocks and logs, even tree stumps covered with green moss, but none of them are the right size. Just when it looks as if we're out of luck, I hear Adam yelling to come deeper into the woods.

"C'mon," Andrew yelps, and we run to find him.

He's kneeling at the far end of an old wood pile, most of it rotted and covered with fungus. Adam uses one foot to roll an old log over, exposing a mess of insects--beetles, ants and centipedes--which scramble for cover.

"How about this? Think it would work?"

"I forgot about this wood," Andrew admits. "My dad chopped it a few years ago and I was supposed to bring it into the shed."

The Wylers have a big wood stove in their family room that goes practically non-stop all winter. It makes the house smell nice and smoky and it's warm in there even on the coldest days.

"Sure," Pete says, "that'll work. Grab a piece of plywood and we'll load it on, otherwise it'd be impossible to carry."

Even using the plywood it's rough going because the log keeps rolling off to one side. We take turns holding it in place and finally make it down to the tunnel opening. It's amazing, but we've done such a good job of hiding the serpent that even I have a hard time finding where it begins and ends. If we have a hard time knowing where it is no one else will ever find it.

"I'll bring candles tomorrow," Strat says. "I only hope there's enough oxygen in there to keep them burning and us breathing." He stares at Andrew, who stares at the ground. "How do worms breathe, anyway?"

Is Strat just being crazy, or has he found out about Andrew's asthma? Unless he and Taylor found that diary there's no way they could know.

"You never heard of worm breath?" Adam says before Andrew has a chance to tell him the great Darwin discovered they breathe through their skin. I step forward quickly and lay my arm across his back.

"Hey, what time are we doing this anyway?" I ask to change the subject. "How about getting it over with right after lunch?"

"Too early, Wills," Strat says, turning to me. I can see my reflection in his pupils, and I'm about as big as an ant. "Initiation's got to be closer to dusk. We want it to be dark, almost black, out. It's a critical part of the ritual."

"W-w-what ritual?" Pete stammers. Behind his big thick glasses he's blinking like crazy.

Strat doesn't take his eyes off me as he answers.

"Initiation," he says slowly. "Crawling through the tunnel in broad daylight would be easy, way too easy. Darkness makes it somewhat more challenging."

Nobody says anything and I keep my mouth shut. I don't like the idea of coming up here in the dark but I don't want to be the wimp who admits that. Strat looks pleased he has successfully freaked us all out, I can tell, so I decide to call his bluff.

"Fine. Five o'clock all right?"

Andrew raises his eyebrows.

"Six." Strat says. "Maybe we should make it seven. The later the better."

Why not make it midnight, I wonder, but I keep quiet. Six o'clock in the woods will be plenty dark, and sarcasm has already gotten me into trouble once.

"Fine. We'll meet here at six sharp. Bring flashlights if you need them."

"We won't, but you kids might," Taylor says as he and Strat start to leave.

The butt of Strat's shovel catches Andrew in the back when he turns, making him pitch forward and lose his balance. He goes down, putting his arms out to break his fall so it isn't as bad as it looks. Adam and I scramble to help. His arm is cut from being jabbed by a stick, and a bright, red bubble of blood appears almost immediately.

Colin whips out a bandana.

"Here," he says, handing it to Andrew. "Use this."

The sound of Strat's laughter floats back through the trees.

"Listen, it's the boogeyman," I say.

Andrew looks up.

"Shapeshifters," he says. "Forces of darkness in human form."

Pete coughs a few times.

"I don't like it," he says to me, his voice low and shaky.

I know what he means but I play dumb.

"You don't like what?"

The red spot on Colin's bandana is getting bigger. Pete holds his hands out, palms up, arms opened wide.

"Any of it. This whole thing. I mean, we're in much deeper than we should be, including Strat and Taylor in the club and having this stupid initiation. And now we're doing it at night. This is crazy! It'll be impossible to see and one of us could get stuck. I'm just not sure I want to go through with it, that's all."

Somewhere high above us a woodpecker starts drilling into a tree, the rat-a-tat-tat of his beak echoing sharply against the bark like a machine gun. I look up but can't see him anywhere.

"It's too late," Andrew says simply, "we have to."

He clamps one hand over the cloth on his arm, keeping the pressure on.

"Let me see that," I say. "It must be deep or it would have stopped."

Andrew jerks his arm away from me. The last thing he wants is for this to turn into a big deal.

"Cut it out, Wills," he says. "A little bleeding never killed anyone."

"That's what you think," Pete says.

We watch in the growing darkness as the circle of blood claims more of the bandana than one little cut should.

# Chapter Sixteen

To celebrate the end of school Andrew sleeps over on Thursday. We drag our sleeping bags down into the basement to get as far away from Taylor as possible. Not that it matters much, because he and Strat are at a dance at the Junior High. Connie has gone too, but not with them.

"Poor Connie," Andrew says.

We're eating popcorn and watching a James Bond video. Andrew and I love Bond movies, the guy is so cool. Right now he's wrestling some bald-headed muscle man on the edge of a cliff and it looks as if he's going over, because Bond is not nearly as big as the bad guy. Every time he's trembling on the brink, the sweat shining on his muscled arms, he gets a break at the very last second and rolls away to safety.

"Huh?" I ask, not taking my eyes off the screen. "Why poor Connie?"

Andrew tilts his head back and shoves a fistful of popcorn into his mouth. For a skinny guy he sure eats a lot.

"You know, going to that dance full of sweaty boys who want to jump on her," he mumbles, his mouth full. "It can't be any fun." I wonder if he realizes that he's one of those boys.

Earlier tonight Taylor and Connie had a big fight when she needed to get into the bathroom and he was hogging it, trying to shave and cutting himself badly in the process. When he came out of the bathroom there were little pieces of toilet paper pasted on the wounds spread around his face and neck.

"Nice," I told him. "The girls are going to love that. That polka dot look is so in."

I ducked into my room but he just stormed across the hall and slammed the door.

Connie must have tried on a hundred outfits. Her bed was piled high. When she finally came down she was in some red dress that hung low on her shoulders. Her dark hair was gathered high on her head and pinned. She looked great. Strat, who'd been hanging out with my father in the living room, making small talk and waiting for Taylor, almost passed out when he saw her.

"Don't worry about Connie, she can take care of herself," I tell Andrew. He's probably going to have some crazy dreams tonight, with earthworms attacking any guy who has the nerve to dance with her. I'll hear all the gory details in the morning, I'm sure.

"It isn't Connie I feel sorry for, actually, it's the poor creature Taylor gets dazzled by. He'll probably drool all over her and sweat up a storm. Hope his deodorant works."

Both of us concentrate on the movie for a moment, thinking about this. Taylor wears some heavy duty musk deodorant that stinks up a room when he enters. Though he swears it's a babe magnet, I have my doubts.

"Think he'll put the moves on anyone?" Andrew asks. A couple of whole kernels fall to the floor.

I shrug. It's a horrible but fascinating thought.

"Only if she's blind," I say and we crack up.

Andrew touches my arm and points to the screen. Bond has escaped from the ripped muscle man and is lying on a beach with some blond beauty who isn't wearing much for a bathing suit. She's running her fingers through Bond's hair and wrapping her long, tan legs around his. Each time the waves crash in, they just miss getting Bond wet. His hair, slickly combed back, is never disturbed. Hers looks like someone has been sleeping in it.

"Oh, man," Andrew breathes.

These scenes really get to him. They have the opposite effect on me so I start to giggle. Andrew completely misses his mouth with the popcorn and he starts laughing too. The door at the top of the stairs opens and my mother comes halfway down to say goodnight. She is the complete opposite of a Bond babe in her fuzzy bathrobe and hair drawn back into a messy ponytail. The eye goo she's wearing hasn't been thoroughly rubbed in and honestly, she looks like a raccoon.

"What's so funny?" she asks.

I raise myself up on one elbow and look at Andrew.

"We were just thinking of Taylor at the dance and pitying his victims," I say. It's not a complete lie.

Andrew smiles. My mother shakes her head, but she's smiling, too.

"Wait'll you get there," she says. "It's not so easy. Is the movie almost over?"

"In about ten minutes."

"Daddy and I are going to bed now. It's late. Turn out the lights at a reasonable hour and get some sleep."

"Yeah, Ma, right."

"Night, Mrs. Peterson," Andrew says. "Thanks."

It's a little bit of a downer to have your mother come in looking like that right in the middle of a key scene but what can I do about it? After she leaves Bond gets rid of the bad guys, leaves the babe broken-hearted, and speeds away in this unbelievably hot red sports car. We lie in the dark and talk for a while. It has been a long week, I'm really tired. The end of school is always hard for me. It's something I look forward to, but it's bittersweet because I know that next year, the work will be even harder. Just when I'm getting comfortable in one grade I get tossed up into another.

We decide to try and stay awake until Taylor and Connie come in. It's Andrew's idea. He doesn't want to fall asleep until he knows she's home safe.

"You worried about tomorrow?" I ask.

The light from the DVD player is still on so I crawl halfway out of my sleeping bag and shut it off.

"Kinda. You?"

"Yeah. I wish Strat was going first, not last. I don't like the idea of all of us in there, on top of each other in the dark, with him outside. How do we know he isn't going to pull something funny? And he's the oldest, if anyone has to be sacrificed it should be him."

89

"Yeah," Andrew says, half asleep.

I lie there thinking about the tunnel, about how much easier this would all be if we really were worms. Imagine if we could be like a comic book hero, half worm, half man.

"If we were worms, initiation would be a piece of cake."

Andrew's soft laughter drifts across the darkness at me, and then I must have fallen asleep, because the next thing I know it's morning. A light rain is falling when we get up and it seems as if both Connie and Taylor had fun because at ten o'clock they're still in bed. Andrew and I kill some time playing computer games and shooting hoops, trying to figure out what to do with the rest of the day.

"If it's raining we won't have initiation, right?" Andrew asks.

I'm right there with him, I'd like to skip it too but the rain seems to be letting up as a dense, gray fog replaces it.

"Good try," I say. "It's supposed to stop by lunchtime."

We go over to his house for a while and make ourselves lunch. Mrs. Wyler wraps some carrot peelings and a mess of stuff in a wet paper towel for the worms. When we get up to the club Andrew takes the top off the tank and sprinkles it in. Most of the food we'd thrown in earlier in the week has disappeared.

"Do you have to turn the soil or anything?"

"I don't think so," he says. "They seem to have eaten all this other stuff okay. They really like this junk, they thrive on it."

I notice a few worms pressed up against the sides, not moving. It looks as if maybe things are getting crowded in there so I tell Andrew.

"Yeah, well, I'm supposed to thin them out every so often, which is a good sign. It means they're breeding."

We look at each other.

"The sex life of a worm," I breathe, "pretty hot stuff."

Andrew taps the side of the tank but they don't move. They don't even wave.

"Maybe they're busy," I say.

Andrew sits back on his heels.

"I got an A on my science project. Mr. Abbot really liked it. He said he could tell I'd done a ton of research, and that using worms to convert garbage into fertilizer had great potential."

I didn't know the part about using the worms to make fertilizer but knew from the start that Abbot would like his project. Andrew is really involved with the science club and Abbot is their advisor. So getting a high grade on his project seems like a slam dunk from the start.

"Well, he's right, you did do a ton of research. If old Darwin was still kicking you probably would have interviewed him. And think about it, some extra investigative work will take place tonight at the serpent."

Andrew gets off his heels and sits on the floor, wrapping his arms around his knees. Outside the rain is running down the windows in uneven silver streams.

"I had a dream about tonight last night," he says.

Instead of moaning, which will set him off, I control myself and close my eyes.

"Yeah?"

"It was freaky, actually, it was really scary."

I open my eyes. He isn't kidding.

"What happened?"

"We were all up at the serpent. I'm pretty sure it was dark, but it was kind of hard to tell. Adam and Pete and everybody else went first, down into the hole, and I was left alone outside, in the woods."

"The opposite of sardines," I say. "Where was I?"

He just waves his hand at me.

"Nobody made any noise, it was completely quiet so I couldn't tell when they'd made it into the chamber, or how far into the tunnel they went. I couldn't see Strat, but I could hear him laughing, you know, that big, deep obnoxious noise he makes..."

"Yeah, right, go on," I say.

91

"He must have been behind the pines or something, he wasn't in there with the rest of you. Anyway, I didn't want to crawl in, but knew I had to."

Andrew lowers his forehead into his arms so I can't see his face.

"Okay, so then what?"

"Halfway through I got stuck, and I freaked. It was pitch black. I felt around in the dirt, because something sharp was lying under me. It was Pete's glasses. Only they were all twisted and smashed, like they'd been run over or something. It was hard to recognize what they were, but when I realized they were his glasses I started screaming, and then I woke up in your basement."

Andrew looks up, blinking, all pale and shaken as if he has just seen a ghost. Actually, I'm relieved it wasn't worse, but I reach over and touch his arm.

"Yeah, well, I've got news for you. It was all in your head," I say. "You're the one who's always telling me how much you love nightmares, how exciting they are. Now you have a good one, first class, and you're all freaked out."

I give a little laugh, more like a cough, but Andrew doesn't smile. He is right on the verge of psyching himself out about tonight.

"This whole club was your idea. The Annelids were going to rule, remember? Initiation to weed out the weak from the strong, right? We were going to outsmart the bullies, use our brains to drain their brawn. Well, guess what? It's too late, you're in too deep. You can't back away, dream or no dream. If you wimp out this club will be ruined and Strat will harass you the rest of your life!"

I get up and stand over him. Andrew's head is buried in his arms again but I feel no sympathy. He created this monster and now he wants out. I wait there a minute, but he doesn't respond and doesn't look up. He knows I'm right. We both know he's scared, and fear is contagious. That's the part I don't like.

"Don't be a wimp," I say. "Get some rest this afternoon, you're going to need it. I'll stop by tonight at around quarter to six."

Outside the rain has stopped again and the sky seems to be brightening. Maybe by tonight it'll be clear, with a full moon or something, and we can get this whole thing over with. I'll feel better when it's history. Trotting towards the path I come upon a small pile of Barney's manure, fresh and still slightly steaming. I give one hard, well-aimed kick and it flies apart in all directions.

"The sheet," I say aloud although there's no one around to hear, "has hit the fan."

# Chapter Seventeen

"In some parts of the world, people eat worms," Andrew tells us as he, Pete, Colin and I walk through the pasture and into the woods on Friday evening. Apparently he has recovered from being freaked out by last night's dream and is ready for action.

"Gross," Colin moans, clutching his sides. "I don't want to hear about it!"

It doesn't take a lot to make Colin throw up, he's a pro at it. On field trips this year he could never take the bus ride. His mother sends him with a little brown paper bag just like that one they give you when you go on a plane. I move away from him now just in case he decides to hurl. Andrew, however, is pleased and actually encouraged by his reaction.

"Well, for one thing, they're full of protein," he says cheerfully. "In a lot of third world countries meat is scarce. Think about it, worms are plentiful and practically free."

"Practically?" I ask. "When was the last time you paid for worm meat?"

The woods are still lit by the last rays of the sun and a good breeze is blowing. All the clouds have disappeared. The sky is clear, beautiful in that peculiar way it glows after it has been raining. It's like the world has been cleaned up and left sparkling.

"Strat's gonna be pissed that it is almost six and still light," I say. I'm feeling pretty good about the evening, thinking it may even be fun. Maybe we can get this whole initiation thing over in about an hour and be home by dark. Then next week we can figure out how many more kids we'll want in the club and really get things started.

I'm wearing my oldest stained jeans and my tee shirt is ripped under one arm. We're all in ratty clothes, perfect for the job ahead. Andrew's jeans look as if they've been ironed. They've got a neat crease down the middle which we've already razzed him about. He claims the crease stays there on its own, even after multiple washings.

"Yeah," Pete says to me. "Strat forgot the days are getting longer. It's June. There should be plenty of light for a while at least."

Pete's all dressed in black. He looks a little sinister, a little less nerdy. I think being part of the Annelid Club is doing things for him. Using his design to build the tunnel, then joining together to outsmart Taylor and Strat by getting them to do most of the digging, has given us a bit of an advantage. Andrew told us that Darwin studied worms to see how much mental strength they displayed. Being in the Annelid Club has tested our mental power, too, with the big test, initiation, coming tonight. It's kind of amazing how this has all evolved. Maybe the whole thing wasn't such a wild idea after all. And maybe this summer will be the best ever.

"Yes!" I say loudly. "Annelids rule!"

Pete grins and flashes me a thumbs up.

"I don't know, we shouldn't be so worried about doing this initiation stuff in the dark," Andrew says. "It's kind of a natural thing, when you think of it. Worms are nocturnal, so it is probably their favorite time. That's when they do all their serious work. They don't even have eyes but they can distinguish dark from light."

"Nice," I say, "that's very comforting. Strat and Taylor will be thrilled to hear it."

"Darkness from light, good from evil, this has all the ingredients of a good mystery," Colin adds. He kind of dances sideways ahead of us as if he can't get to the serpent fast enough.

"Yeah, and we know which part those two goons would play," I say. It's a powerful feeling to think we can outsmart my brother and Strat.

Up ahead lies the serpent, where Adam, Strat and Taylor are already waiting. Strat is wearing his cowboy boots and dark gloves. Both he and Taylor have black knit caps pulled down over their ears. They look ready to rob a bank, or find work as undertakers. Either way, they're hired.

"You expecting a storm?" I ask as we arrive.

Taylor swings out to cuff my head but I'm ready. I duck and his fist slices the air.

"I was just telling these guys that in some undeveloped parts of the world people eat worms," Andrew says. "I brought some along because I thought it would be good karma before we begin initiation."

Andrew is always talking about karma. It's what your fate or destiny is and he considers it right up there alongside dreams in importance.

"Karma?" Strat says.

He screws up his face, an indicator there's actually some brain activity underway. Clearly he has no idea what Andrew is talking about. He looks at Taylor for translation.

Taylor shrugs.

"I don't know, it's some kind of Buddhist junk that says if you do something in life it can influence what happens to you later."

I'm actually impressed, because that's a pretty fair description.

Taylor snorts, letting Strat know he thinks the whole thing is ridiculous.

"Only nuts believe that stuff," Strat says. "Right?"

Andrew slides a small backpack off his shoulders and takes a box out. He opens it, reaches in, and pulls out a handful of Gummy worms. They're neon red, orange, yellow, even lime green. If they weren't such bizarre colors they'd look like the real thing, but instead they look like they're made out of rubber. He picks one and ceremoniously lowers it into his open mouth, letting the end dangle as he chews. My brother holds his hand out and Andrew passes him the box.

This worm eating ritual is a nice touch. I have to hand it to him. Once again he has control and has taken Strat and Taylor

97

by surprise. Taylor's eyes are closed and worm ends are dangling from his mouth, too. His cheeks are full and a bright orange bubble of saliva forms between his lips. Andrew looks quickly from him to me and smiles. Pete blinks hard when he chews. He looks ready to bolt as soon as he's finished. We've postponed our descent into the tunnel with this strange meal. That can only be a good thing.

Overhead the pines make a soft, moaning sound as the breeze lifts Andrew's hair off his forehead. The setting sun blinks from behind the trees and it isn't quite as warm as it was. I shiver a little, thinking that if this weird business is going to move forward we might as well get moving. I'd like to be home before midnight.

"Worms may have small brains," Andrew says, breaking the silence, "but they do have five hearts."

This bizarre fact snaps Strat out of his calming karma trance. He grabs the nearly empty box from Andrew's hands and throws it to the ground, grinding it into the soil with his boot.

"Enough already! Shut up about the friggin worms!" he growls. "I have a special little initiation of my own planned for tonight, something I think you boys will enjoy. Taylor?"

My brother stumbles over to him, holding out his knapsack like some kind of offering to the gods. Taylor's face looks kind of pale so I'm thinking he's either feeling lousy or this surprise isn't going to be fun. Strat takes the knapsack and pulls out a small coffee can and a plastic bag filled with earthworms, real ones. He arranges some sticks together over crumpled newspaper, takes out a lighter, and then feeds the fire with bigger sticks until it catches and blazes up brightly.

Andrew shifts his weight from one foot to the other.

"Hey, what are you doing?" he asks.

Strat places the can on the fire, opens the bag, and drops the worms in, one by one. They make a sickening, popping noise as they hit the hot metal and an acrid smell of burning flesh fills the air. Pete looks as if he is about to hurl and I carefully avoid looking at Colin. If one of us starts it'll be like a chain reaction, everybody vomiting into the fire.

Next Strat pulls out a paper napkin and dumps a couple of charred worms into it. Their bodies are black and stiff and barely recognizable. He holds this out to Pete, who steps back, stumbling, his hand over his mouth.

"No way," he says. "Not doing it." He backs away even further.

"Eat it!" Strat barks, "It's part of the initiation. If you don't eat them, you're out."

Pete looks around for help. I know I should say something, somebody should, but we're all afraid to. He closes his eyes and quickly crams the whole mess into his mouth. I have to turn away as he chews or get sick myself. I can't even look at Pete, in fact, I can't really look at anyone.

"Tasty?"

Strat's booming laugh is joined by Taylor's, which comes out kind of weak in comparison, but nobody else is amused.

"Cut it out!" I say, too loudly, and kick the coffee can off the fire.

Sparks fly up as it falls sideways and some of the charred worms spill out into the dirt. One spark lands in some leaves. In a flash Adam moves over and stamps it out with his foot.

"Ouch! Getting a little touchy, Willsy?" Strat says. "Aren't we all having fun? No? Well then, okay, the cocktail party is over. Let's get started on the real test. Who goes first? Petey?"

Strat has a sick little smirk on his face which widens after Taylor pushes Pete forward. Pete turns and spits several times onto the forest floor, trying to remove any remnants of the bizarre meal from his mouth. A brown string of charred worm hangs from his lips. The rest of us stand there helpless, sorry for the things he's been forced to do. First the disgusting meal and now the descent into darkness. Pete is getting a raw deal here.

He wipes his mouth clean with his sleeve and steps forward, his hands up to his face, palms pressed together as if in prayer. I touch his shoulder.

"Want me to hold on to your glasses? We could put them on that log over there till you come out."

Pete leans over, his breath warm on my ear.

"I'm not sure I can make it," he whispers. "I can't see without them."

Taylor hears this and gives a loud hoot.

"It's dark in there, Pete," he says sweetly. "There's nothing **to** see."

He reaches over to remove the glasses, but I'm faster. I knock his arm away, and he punches me, catching me on the shoulder this time.

"You're such a jerk! Leave him alone," I say.

"Ok, mom, have it your way," Taylor says.

He laughs and steps aside, making a sweeping motion towards the tunnel entrance with his arms. Pete takes two small steps forward and stops.

"W-w-what about the candles, the light?" he asks.

"What about them?" says Strat.

"I th-thought they were going to be in there, in the tunnel. How will we see?"

"Who says they aren't?" Taylor says, coming up alongside Strat.

Instantly we know they must already have put the candles in without us. It must have been done last night, with just the two of them. If there are any more surprises tonight it'll be because Strat and Taylor planned them. The rest of us are coming to this cold. Andrew looks over at me in alarm. How could we have let this happen?

Pete sort of sags against me.

"I really don't want to do this," he mumbles, loud enough for me to hear.

I don't either, I'm right there with him, but I have no idea how to get out of it. Most times when you play with something, and then you don't want to play anymore, you stop. This time we're on some kind of sick conveyor belt going forward whether we like it or not. Chickening out is not an option, not now.

A twig snaps as Strat steps up beside us and reaches into his pocket. He holds up a knife and there's a tiny, hissing noise as he pushes a button and a slim silver blade flashes out. We all look at the thing, but even after seeing it our brains don't immediately process what he's holding. Nobody moves.

"I carry this little friend around in case I need it," Strat says quietly, "and I'm thinking now's the perfect time to use it. The Annelid club isn't for wimps, remember? Our goal is to weed out the weak from the strong, am I right? We dug the tunnel and now we have to crawl our way to the end. That's what this initiation is about. I didn't write the rules, we all agreed to them."

"You're insane," I say. "You're totally out of your mind."

Strat doesn't answer, he just presses the switchblade against his thumb as if testing it, a smile spreading slowly across his face. Pete looks as if he is about to pass out. Going down into the tunnel might be better than staying up here dealing with Strat. I glance over at Taylor, but he is gazing off into the woods as if none of this is happening. I'm pretty sure switchblades are illegal, so I'm wondering if my brother even knew Strat had one. Taylor might be dumb, but he's not dangerous. The stakes of this game are changing faster than we can keep up. One of us should put a stop to the craziness, but the moment to do so has passed.

"It'll be OK, Pete. You won't be alone. We'll all be coming in right there behind you," I say quickly. "We're Annelids, we're all in it together and we're doing this for the club."

That sounds stupid, even to me, but I can't think of anything else to say. I wrap my arms around myself and squeeze, hard. The light is fading now but there aren't any fireflies yet. Maybe it isn't dark enough, either that or it's too early in summer. Why can't I remember when fireflies first appear?

"You made your point," I tell Strat. "Put that thing away."
He looks at me, still smiling.

"Say please."

"Please."

My voice is so soft I barely hear myself, but in one easy motion Strat slides the blade down into the handle and slips it into his back pocket. Pete straightens up. He pushes his glasses back up on his face and breathes deeply.

"The Annelids, right," he says, then crouches down on his knees and slides down into the tunnel opening, pulling himself along with effort until the soles of his sneakers disappear at last. Pieces of dirt on the sides comes loose and fall into the hole but generally the thing holds up pretty well. It'll probably need some repair tomorrow after initiation is over, if we ever want to come near it again, that is.

"One down, six to go," Taylor says.

# Chapter Eighteen

We stand around the opening listening for sounds of Pete's progress but all we hear is the wind moving through the trees. I check for a moon. Nothing, maybe it's still too early. It would be nice to be able to hear Pete, to get some sign he has made it into the chamber.

I crouch down by the opening, cupping my hands around my mouth.

"Pete!"

Nobody moves.

"Yo, Pete!"

"Maybe he can't hear us," Adam says softly.

Somewhere deep in the woods an owl starts hooting. Owls and worms, we're out here with all the night creatures.

"Fine, who's next?" Strat asks. He stands there with this stupid smile, his arms crossed tightly against his chest.

He knows perfectly well that Adam is next, we all do.

"Do me a favor. When you get in there, yell or make noise or something so we know you've made it," I say to Adam.

"Don't forget to leave the lights on for us," Taylor says.

Adam nods, then slides quickly down into the tunnel. Aside from his grunting and the scraping noises his boots make we don't hear much. Colin's got a flashlight that he flicks on and points at the entrance. More dirt has fallen, and there is a deep gouge on one side where Adam's boots took out some earth. The serpent looks even less inviting at night than it did by day.

"Taylor?"

I look over at him. It's his turn, and he isn't exactly rushing in. He shrugs and steps up to the hole.

"I'll go when I'm ready," he sniffs. Then he just stands there looking at the tunnel.

I know my brother and I think he's afraid. It's weird, because all of a sudden I feel sorry for him, and have to fight the urge to go over and put an arm around his shoulder. I know he'd punch me if I did that, so I don't move. Just then we hear a muffled shout coming from somewhere down where the end of the tunnel should be.

"Adam!" I yell.

"Adam or Pete, take your pick," Taylor says, and plunges in.

He's bigger and wider than the rest of us, except Strat, so it seems to take him longer to vanish than it took the other two. He's also louder. We hear a lot of scraping, shuffling sounds, and he keeps grunting as he inches his way along. He takes more dirt with him than the other two have, it comes off both sides and falls into the opening. By now I'm sorry I wasn't the first one to go. It's murder standing around out here, waiting to be next.

Andrew moves up beside me. He's breathing a little hard and fast for someone who has been standing still. I wonder if he brought that inhaler stuff he needs for his asthma, if it's inside his knapsack. I don't ask, though, because if he hasn't, I don't want to know.

"Courage," he whispers. I nod.

His pale face peers out at me from the dark. For a moment I'm sad we made fun of his creased jeans earlier. It doesn't really matter, none of that seems important now. I almost tell him but I don't trust my voice.

Strat reaches out and grabs Colin's flashlight, shining it up his nose. His nostrils light up like tiny pink shells and his eyes glitter.

"Wills!" he booms.

He looks like some freak in a horror movie but I don't let him psych me out. Not now. I'm determined that he not know I'm rattled. Besides, I'd rather he concentrate on bothering me and leave Andrew alone.

"Lovely," I say, "very pretty." I tuck my head, stretch my arms out in front of me and follow the others into the black hole.

The earth is damp from all the rain. It smells moist and familiar, like something I've been used to smelling all my life.

But the darkness is so complete it takes me by surprise even though I've been expecting it. I close my eyes tightly and focus on reaching out my arms as far as they'll extend as I drag myself forward. Once or twice I forget to hold my head up and get a face full of dirt as punishment.

I'm not too far into the thing before I spot the first candle, its small yellow flame flickering unsteadily in the tunnel's draft. Somebody, either my brother or Strat, has carved a hollow place out of the wall and secured the candle inside. Instead of being comforting, the light has the opposite effect, illuminating only a small part of the way and leaving the rest dark. Wax is dripping down one side and spilling over onto the walls.

With or without the light, you've got to have faith that pulling yourself through this black cave will bring you somewhere, that you're not stuck in here forever. Andrew will appreciate this part of this crazy initiation because it's almost a nightmare come true.

I stop pulling myself forward to rest a minute before continuing to drag my body toward the chamber. It's impossible to turn back even if I wanted to. The only way to go is forward.

At the second candle I cross my hands and put my face on them. There isn't a lot of air in here. Making any kind of progress is hard work. If worms are nocturnal, there must be hundreds of them monitoring my clumsy maneuverings. They don't have eyes, but Andrew said they sense movement through earth vibrations. I remember he told me that Darwin discovered this crazy fact after someone played a piano near them.

With me in here they must think a giant is invading their turf because my struggle to move through the tunnel must be producing massive shock waves. Suddenly I feel a surge of panic, like maybe I'll never see daylight or the sun again, so I start crawling again with new energy.

"Wills!"

Adam's voice comes to me through the darkness. It doesn't sound so far away.

"Yeah, Adam. Almost there!"

105

With huge effort I scramble forward, pulling myself along with my elbows. When my fingers touch somebody's leg, hands reach out and grab my arms, dragging me through the dirt and into the chamber. Two candles, one on either side of the hollowed out room, throw just enough light for me to see faces. Almost everyone looks as if they've been eating a little dirt the way I have, but that's about the worst of it.

"You made it!" Adam says.

I slide my legs under me and sit up, amazed at how big the space that we've carved looks once I'm fully inside.

"What do you know, Wills," Taylor says. His voice is flat, without emotion, and he's sitting with his legs curled up to his chest, his arms wrapped around them. He's hunched over with his head tucked because sitting up would mean it would hit the roof.

This is the nearest thing to praise my brother has said to me in ten years. He didn't shove me and he didn't call me stupid. He must be some kind of freaked out. I search for his face in the darkness but he's sitting across from me so I can't really read his expression.

"Yeah, I made it," I pant. "Where's Pete?"

"Over here," Pete answers. His voice is low and soft.

"Your glasses all right?" I ask.

"Yeah."

Just then we hear someone, it must be Colin, crawling slowly towards us. From the sounds of it he's struggling.

"Colin!" I yell, "Keep coming! You're almost there!" I lean towards the noise and grab hold of him as soon as his arm reaches through the opening. He's breathing hard and he kind of hugs me for a second before letting go.

"It's okay, you made it."

"I didn't think I could," Colin says.

He sounds shaky, like he could be close to tears. I'm glad we're in the semi darkness, and I'm sure that if we could see each other we'd all look a little freaked out. Being in here is really creepy. We'd underestimated that. It's like you can hardly remember what the sun looks like, or trees, or grass, or flowers. The only reality is the cool, damp earth, the near total darkness, and the silence.

Then I remember that Andrew goes next. I stare hard at the spot in the wall where I think the opening is but of course there's nothing to see. It feels as if we've been stuck in this tunnel for hours.

My brother starts to whistle, a thin, soft sound that's oddly comforting and irritating at the same time.

"Man!" he says when he stops, "I'll be glad to get out of here."

"Me too," Adam says. "Who knew the night could be so dark?"

Cavemen knew, I think, that's why they invented fire. It sounds like something Andrew would say, but before I can speak I hear something really alarming. There's a frantic, steady coughing coming from somewhere deep in the tunnel. It's sort of muffled, but definitely human.

"What's that?" Colin asks.

"You mean, who's that?" Adam says.

"Shhh!" I hiss.

We strain to hear more, and it's quiet for a few seconds, then the coughing starts again, more intensely this time. I get on my hands and knees and crawl blindly towards the opening, bumping into Colin as I do.

"Hey, Wills, watch it!" he says.

I crawl over him, reaching my hands out to feel the hole in the earth that marks the opening into the tunnel.

"Sorry, but I think he's in trouble. Andrew! Keep crawling, buddy, you're almost there."

We hear him struggling to move forward, his boots or sneakers or whatever he's wearing knocking against the side of the walls. I lie on my stomach and thrust one arm deep into the tunnel as far as it'll go. He's gasping for air, making that odd, wheezing noise he made on the playground. Hearing it again gives me the creeps--it's got to be one of the worst sounds I've ever heard. If he had to fight so hard for air on the playground how's he going to be able to breathe down here?

"Andrew!" I start crawling crazily back towards the entrance.

Behind me, Taylor lunges forward trying to grab my feet to prevent me from going.

"Are you insane, Wills? What are you doing?" he yells, but I ignore him.

Andrew is fighting for breath, big time. My own chest tightens in sympathy--I wish I could breathe for him. I push myself to move faster, to find him. I scramble forward through the dirt faster than I'd thought possible, and when I finally touch him, I sob and grab his shoulders. Pulling him toward me I start to slowly back up. It's difficult because I keep knocking against the tunnel walls and can't get in position to really pull. He's wheezing and sputtering and I'm not sure he even knows I'm there.

"Andrew, hold on!" I half sob, tears stinging my eyes. Talking exhausts me, so I just make grunting noises as I move backwards, holding on to him so hard I'm afraid I'll break his bones. I worry that if I lose my grip, he'll sink away from me into the blackness. Even if I can pull him to the chamber I don't have his inhaler. Dragging him is painfully slow, it takes great effort to move just a few inches, and I'm not sure how long he can hold on. It's hard work keeping his face up off the dirt floor and I can't even tell if he's still breathing.

"Help!" I cry out when my feet finally hit the cleared space of the chamber. "Move over, everyone! Give him room!"

They press close together to make space for us.

"Wills, what the...?"

Taylor doesn't finish his sentence because I don't let him. Andrew's breath is coming in thin, rattling gasps, and he doesn't move. He's lying on the dirt, bent over because there isn't really space for him to do anything else. There's no room in the chamber to sit him up, turn him around, or try to help him breathe. There's not room for anything.

I wipe my sleeve against my face, realizing I must have been blubbering when it comes back wet.

"Guys, this is an emergency," I say, sounding calm. Even though I feel shaky, my voice surprises me. "We've got to lie on our backs and use our feet to kick the roof off this thing. Andrew's in big trouble, he can't breathe, and we've got to get him out of here, now!"

I lie back as well as I can and put my feet up against the roof. Colin and Adam do too. Somebody's whimpering softly, it must be Pete, against the back wall. The three of us position ourselves, on our backs, to kick the roof off. Andrew just lies there, still as death.

"One, two, three kick!" I yell, and push up with all my strength. Dirt rains down around us, but the ceiling doesn't budge. Pete crosses his arms, leans over and covers Andrew's face so the falling dirt won't hurt him. Taylor lies back alongside Adam, feet in the air.

"Push," he grunts, "again!"

We push again, harder this time and all together. This time the boards lift a little then come back down again. More dirt rains down around us, onto our hair and faces, but I don't care.

"One, two, three again!" I yell, and this time the boards lift up enough for me to reach one arm out and push them aside. Taylor and Adam help and together we manage to move enough of the roof to one side so we can stand up. Most of the dirt and leaves on top fall in when we shift the boards, but just seeing the sky is such a relief I feel weak in the knees. The night is still and there the moon is, a hazy ring behind the clouds. Taylor climbs quickly out and reaches his arms in so he can help drag Andrew up and onto the ground.

"Lift him up so I can grab him." Taylor is the only one of us strong enough to do this.

"Adam," I say, "I'm going to need your help. Take Andrew under one arm and I'll get the other. He's going to be heavy, but we need to get him up and out of here."

Adam grabs Andrew on one side, I take the other. Colin gets him around the waist. We fumble a lot, and it's sloppy, but within minutes we're able to lift him up far enough for Taylor to pull him out. For once in my life I'm glad my brother is bigger and stronger than I am.

"Put him on the ground!" I yell.

I can hardly breathe, and now my face is completely wet, so I must be bawling. One by one we heave ourselves up and out of the chamber into the night. Some of the boards and most of the dirt and branches on top fall back into the chamber. The air smells sweet and innocent and faintly of smoke.

Pete's kneeling down beside Andrew's limp body, his head on Andrew's chest. His glasses are sideways on his face, which is streaked with dirt. He looks up at us.

"He's barely breathing!" Pete yells, but I'm already running as fast as I can through the dark woods. Branches slap my face and tear my hair. Even though I've been playing in these woods since I was a little kid, I fall, twice, before I reach the gate to Barney's pasture.

The light glows from the Wylers' kitchen. I reach the stairs, taking them three at a time, and slam against the back door. Mrs. Wyler turns the outside light on. I must look horrible because she moves faster than I've ever seen anyone move.

"Andrew!" she cries, and I collapse in her arms. She knows, even before I can speak.

"He's stuck, back there," I gasp. "He can't breathe."

I feel as if I'm fighting for air, there doesn't seem to be enough of it anywhere.

"Call an ambulance, please!"

I start sobbing as I feel Mr. Wyler's strong arms lift me up and carry me into the kitchen. Everything looks just the way it did before we left this afternoon, but nothing's the same. I hear

Mrs. Wyler on the phone, but I feel like I'm underwater or in shock, because I can't understand anything she says.

Mr. Wyler squats down in front of me.

"Where is he, Wills?" he asks quietly. "Can you take us to him?"

I nod, silently, and sit slumped over in a chair like an old man while they pull flashlights and stuff together. I feel ancient, like this night seems to have lasted for years. By the time the ambulance arrives, throwing pulsating bright lights into the night, illuminating the barn and yard in violent bursts of red, I'm totally numb. The Wylers and two ambulance guys follow me as we run through the pasture and into the woods. I stumble along behind the flashlight's beam as if I've gone without light so long it no longer allows me to see.

When we reach the serpent the others are clustered around Andrew's body. They scatter as we approach. One of the men kneels and fits a white plastic mask over Andrew's face, slipping the cord gently behind his head. They're wearing gloves and they work quickly, hooking him up to a big, green tank. When they lift Andrew's body up onto the stretcher, I'm angry he's so light and small and easily moved. He lies there, perfectly still, the mask covering most of his face. His jeans, still perfectly creased, are covered in dirt.

"Oh my God," Mrs. Wyler sobs, sinking down next to Andrew.

She puts one hand on his forehead and brushes some of the earth off his face. Andrew's dad pulls her up and wraps his arms around her so the men can lift the stretcher. They stumble toward the house, following the ambulance guys and the body of their son. Somebody, Pete I guess, is sitting near the entrance of the tunnel, making small snuffling noises. I brush past him and pick Andrew's backpack up off the ground.

Without the flashlight, the darkness surrounds us again, but none of us makes a move to leave. Maybe it's because we really don't know where to go or what to do. I have no idea where Strat is. I haven't seen him since we crawled into the tunnel. He must have taken off when he heard Andrew in trouble. I wheel around to face Taylor.

"Where's Strat?" I ask. "Where'd he go?"

He shakes his head. I feel belligerent, like I could punch Strat full in the face if he appeared before me now. Suddenly I want to hurt him, to make him pay in some way for what's happened to Andrew.

My brother shrugs.

"Gone," he says.

"Gone?" I repeat. "He never even came into the tunnel! He sent us all in and he didn't have the guts to come in himself?"

I can't believe it. Strat, the oldest and strongest of us, created this monster. He directed the risky initiation, got us into trouble and then he just disappears?

"Took off," Taylor says, his voice flat. "Heard the sirens and just took off."

"Why didn't you follow?" I ask.

Taylor lifts his shoulders.

"You're his sidekick, why didn't you run, too?" I'm so angry I feel like punching my brother. If Strat isn't around maybe he's the next best target.

"Sorry," Taylor mumbles.

He won't meet my eyes, he just stands there, studying the ground. I don't think I've ever heard him say the word before. All of a sudden, I feel exhausted. My body sags and there's not an ounce of fight left in me.

Looking up I see the stars are out in full force, the sky is thick with them. An airplane with blinking red lights moves slowly across it. Taylor comes over and lifts Andrew's backpack off my shoulder.

"C'mon," he says, "Nothing more we can do here. Let's go."

The high, thin wail of a siren pierces the night's silence as we walk home through the dark woods. It's probably the loneliest sound the two of us have ever heard.

# Chapter Nineteen

*Connie.*

When I wake up the next morning, I'm not sure whether I've dreamt about her, or called her name out loud, but when I open my eyes she's sitting in the yellow checked chair directly across from my bed. She's got a thick strand of dark hair wrapped around one finger, with her head tilted to one side, and doesn't immediately notice I'm awake until I stretch my legs out towards the foot of the bed and moan. It must be pretty late because sunlight is flooding my room. Connie looks at me as if expecting me to say something. Maybe I already have.

"What?" I ask.

She crosses and kneels down, reaching out to smooth the hair back off my forehead. She's been doing this ever since we were little and right now it almost makes me cry. Sometimes she treats me like a kid. Sometimes, like now, that feels good.

"I didn't say anything, Wills. I was just waiting for you to wake up. You've been sleeping a long time. Mom sent me up to see if you want any breakfast. In bed."

I smile at her, because all our lives this has been the ultimate treat, breakfast in bed. Then all of a sudden I remember last night, and Andrew. I grunt and push the pillows back so I can sit up. How could I have slept so soundly when he's in the hospital fighting to live?

"Jeez, Connie, last night things got so messed up. Andrew couldn't breathe. He got stuck. In the tunnel. And now he's in the hospital!"

I can't seem to put a complete sentence together so I give up, close my eyes, and try to concentrate. My mouth feels incredibly dry. All I can think about is how badly I want some water. Connie squeezes my hand.

"Shhh, I know. Dad told me what happened. Jeez, Wills, what the heck were you guys doing up there in the woods that late at night? I thought you were all meeting in the barn. Were you having some sort of crazy club party or something? Whatever it was, what happened to Andrew was not your fault. Don't beat yourself up about it. You didn't do anything, how could you have known?"

I shake my head, hard, even before she stops speaking.

"Stop," I protest. She's being nice but I don't deserve it. It only makes me feel worse. "I did, I did know. I knew Andrew had pretty bad asthma, I just didn't think it was that big a deal."

I can see she still doesn't believe me. She thinks I'm in shock or something. I lean forward and pull my hand away.

"Remember Andrew's worm project, the thing he showed you that day in the barn?"

She nods.

"He kept a diary hidden in the barn where the pigeons are. I found it and read all his private stuff. I know that was wrong, but I did it anyway. He'd been to the doctor, he had bad asthma. All the asthma business was in there and he said he'd have to take it easy and really limit his activities. It freaked him out, but he didn't want anyone to know. Even me."

"Kids torture him about so many other things," Connie says sadly.

"Exactly. This was just one more thing they'd use against him. One more weakness to add to the list."

I turn my face toward the wall so Connie won't see my eyes because all of a sudden they sting like crazy.

"But Wills, a lot of kids have asthma, tons of them. I'm sure the Wylers were treating him and it was under control."

I shake my head and study the wallpaper. It's been up for years and the little blue and yellow medallions have faded and worn away in spots. There's a small hole where I must have hung something up a long time ago, the paper torn and jagged around the edges.

"Wrong, Connie. You can die from asthma. I know, we did a respiratory section in science last year and studied all kinds of stuff. People think asthma is harmless but it isn't. I should have known that tunnel was a bad idea, I should have warned him."

Neither of us says anything and I know now she believes me. "Where is he?"

"Still in the hospital. Mrs. Wyler told Dad last night that the first night would be critical. We haven't heard anything yet so I guess that's a good sign."

She doesn't sound convincing and I'm not convinced. Connie rises and pushes the bangs away from her eyes. The two silver bracelets she's wearing slide down her arm and tinkle together like a wind chime.

"I'm going over now. You're in no shape to come, and besides, I can check with the hospital and see if any of us will be let in to see him later. I'll tell Mom you're ready for some breakfast."

"Thanks."

After she leaves I lie in bed for a few minutes, then jump up and start pulling on my jeans. Andrew and I both have the same pair, we put identical patches on one knee. He drew a peace sign on his, I left mine blank so we wouldn't look dumb. Mine's starting to pull away from too many washings. The stuff I wore to the serpent lies on the floor in a dirty heap. I can't even remember having taken it off. Maybe Taylor helped me. I remember him being in my room last night but I don't remember anything else.

By the time my mother knocks I'm putting on my sneakers. The soles are caked with dirt in all the deep grooves and some has dropped in neat little bricks on the floor. I lift the edges of the rug and sweep them under before she opens the door.

"Wills. I brought you something to eat. You must be starving."

My mom looks exhausted, the way she does when she hasn't slept much.

"Ma, you didn't have to do that. I'm up."

I take the tray from her and sit down on the edge of my bed. She sits next to me, fluffs my pillows and lines them up against the headboard.

"C'mon," she says. "Sit back and eat. I didn't bring this all the way up to your room to have you not eat it."

She takes the tray while I slide back against the pillows.

"Have we heard anything?"

She shakes her head.

"Dad and I were there last night with the Wylers but we haven't had word since then. Connie just left for the hospital. She promised she'd call as soon as she gets there."

I stick my spoon into the grapefruit and a small stream of juice shoots out onto my quilt. My mother's made cinnamon toast, my favorite, and hot chocolate with marshmallows. I don't really feel like eating but she'll go crazy if I don't so I cram it into my mouth and concentrate on swallowing. I'm glad to be busy eating because then I don't have to talk. There isn't much right now I feel like saying. There isn't much I could say.

"I wish she'd hurry up and call," I mumble and my mother nods. One nice thing about her, she doesn't ask tons of questions like most mothers. She lets you have some room, lets you sort thoughts out for yourself.

"I know you do, Wills. We all do."

Down the hall I hear Taylor playing some game on the computer. Usually he moans and yells and makes all kinds of painful noise but this morning he's silent. All we hear is a steady succession of bleeps and burps as he works his way through the maze. When the phone finally rings it takes me a minute before I realize it's not part of his game, it's the real thing. My mother jumps up and goes into the hall to answer.

I'm already standing as she returns holding out the phone. "It's Connie."

"Thanks," I say. "Hello?"

"Wills," Connie says, "I'm at the hospital. I talked to Andrew's mom. He just got out of intensive care. He's breathing on his own and they think he's going to be okay."

My knees kind of give out on me and I sink to the floor with my back against the wall.

"Wills? You there? Did you hear me?"

I keep the phone pressed against one ear and stare at the wall. For a split second I think I'm going to start bawling but instead I start laughing. My sister must think I'm cracking up or something, and maybe I am.

"Yeah, Connie, sorry. I'm just so happy," I take a deep breath, "happy to hear that. Please tell the Wylers for me. Can I come see him?"

"Yeah, Wills, that's why I called. They moved Andrew out of the ICU this morning and you'll be allowed in. He's not supposed to have a lot of visitors but the Wylers wanted you to be able to come. They want you to see him. It's okay for you to visit with his parents there."

"Man," I say, "Connie."

I shake my head and stop talking because now I really do feel like crying.

"I know, Wills. We're all relieved. Tell Mom I'm coming home in a bit."

"Sure," I say. "Thanks for calling."

After we hang up I sit still, leaning my head back and closing my eyes. The wall feels hard, and solid, it feels good. I realize I have to pee in a major way so I get up and head to the bathroom. It seems to take hours to get my zipper down and then it's all I can do not to shoot the pee all over the bathroom in some kind of wild celebration. For the second time this morning I start laughing, who knows why, until Taylor comes down the hall and raps loudly on the door.

"Yo, butthead. You losing it or something?"

I zip up, flush, and open the door. Taylor takes a step back, his eyes wide. Before he speaks I grab his shoulders and give him a hug. He actually lets me hold on for a second or two before he peels me off.

"Taylor! Andrew's okay! He's okay! Connie talked to his parents and they say I can go to the hospital and see him."

I hold up my hand so he can slap me five but he flattens against the wall and moves away from me.

"Okay," he says slowly, "I knew he was going to be fine. You got all worked up over nothing."

I know that my brother did not think everything was going to be okay. I know because I saw his face last night when they were taking Andrew to the ambulance. And I know because he told me he was sorry, and stayed with me until we came home and I got into bed. He might even have tucked me in. But if he wants to play the big guy, and continue this charade, what the heck, I'll let him.

I resist the urge to hug him again and instead put my hand on his arm.

"Yeah, well, you're a lot smarter than I am, because I didn't. I seriously thought he was going to die. And I thought we were responsible. Will you take me over there, now?"

Taylor has his learning permit. He loves any excuse to get behind the wheel and practice. My parents want it to take him a long time to get his license so they're making him learn on a stick shift. Being in the car while he's driving is pretty painful, but I'm so happy I'll do anything to see Andrew. My brother looks at me and narrows his eyes.

"Good idea. I'll go ask Mom," he says and hurries to find her.

It doesn't take long before we're settled, me in the back, my mother beside Taylor. She fastens her seatbelt and leans stiffly back against the seat looking as if she's in a jet poised for takeoff. The car jerks and shudders and crawls towards the hospital. We stall completely at the first red light and some guy in back of us leans on his horn.

"Quiet!" Taylor snarls, but I can tell he's nervous. He looks in his rearview mirror every few seconds and keeps turning his head to see who's in back of him.

"Keep your eyes on the road," my mother says. She's got one hand over her eyes so I'm not sure she can even see.

It takes him a few painful minutes to get the car in gear and moving forward. The light turns green, then yellow, then red before it's green again and we roll forward. When we finally reach the parking lot Taylor turns the car off, forgets to press the clutch, and the car makes a small leap forward before it trembles and dies. The front bumper kisses the guard railing, but only lightly. My mother gives a slight gasp and lowers her forehead into her hands.

"What?" Taylor says. "We made it, didn't we?"

My mother and I leave Taylor in the car. Before we've closed the doors he's got earbuds in, listening to music. Inside, we ask about Andrew at the front desk. Riding the elevator up to the fourth floor I smile at everybody. One little old lady holding a bunch of wilted flowers smiles back. She's missing most of her teeth and the ones remaining don't look so hot.

"I'll wait here, you go in first," my mother says. She spots Andrew's mother coming down the hall and goes to meet her.

I ask the pretty nurse at the front desk about Andrew and she directs me to his room. The walls and floors and everything are shiny and white and the place smells like disinfectant. Andrew is in a little room down at the end with some older kid and I have to walk around a white curtain to find him. He's sleeping, hooked up to a machine that's dripping a clear fluid into his arm. The skin around the needle is bandaged but it's all black and blue. All of a sudden I don't feel so cheerful.

Lying there, with his hospital gown kind of twisted around his body, Andrew looks small and pale. His chest rises and falls slightly so I know he's breathing. I sink to my knees next to his bed and touch his arm but he doesn't move. Now that he's not awake I don't know what to do.

"Andrew," I whisper.

I watch the fluid drip from the bag into the clear tubes and into his arm and wonder if it hurts.

"I'm sorry, man. The Annelids, Andrew, look what happened! We messed up. We totally messed up. It was supposed to be fun. You and I had it all figured out. We were going to follow Darwin's lead, maybe even improve on his experiments with the mighty worm, but something went wrong. I knew about your asthma, I did, and I should have stopped you. It's my fault, the club, the tunnel, everything. Colin, Pete, Adam, none of them knew but me. Not even Taylor. I could have changed the game but I went along with it. I'm so sorry."

I lean my face against the side of his bed and fight back tears. I've been blubbering badly, talking nonsense, but aside from the kid on the other side of the room there's no one there to hear me. I'm praying that the kid, whoever he is, is fast asleep.

"Darwin."

I jerk my head up and look around. Andrew's still lying there, eyes closed. Slowly he opens them and looks at me, and a small smile spreads across his face. I don't know whether to laugh, or cry, or hug him, so I just stare.

"I had the best dream," he whispers.

I lean forward because I can't believe what I've just heard.

"Don't talk," I say, because I think that's what an adult would tell him.

"I have another idea." He coughs softly and then closes his eyes.

"Shhhhh," I say, "take it easy."

But Andrew shakes his head and takes a breath. I lean forward even farther to make it easier. I don't want him to talk, but at the same time I'm eager to hear everything he's got to say. Maybe he was clinically dead, went to the other side, and has come back to give me all the details. That happens to some people, maybe it happened to him.

"A club," he says clearly and firmly, turning his head sideways and fixing his big blue eyes on mine. "I have an idea for another club, Wills. Based on the findings of Charles Darwin, remember that guy I told you about?"

I can't believe my ears. The kid goes to hell and back and this is what he wants to talk about?

"Yeah, right, I was just thinking about him," I say. "But we already tried that club, remember?"

Andrew shakes his head from side to side, slowly. Clearly he doesn't want me to talk, just listen.

"Darwin was that biologist from England. You know he studied worms in the mid-1800s. He did tests on them, played music to see if they could hear. Examined their bodies. Discovered they were amazing environmentalists, that they actually cleaned the earth and made it richer."

"Yeah, sure Andrew, I know all that. You've already told me."

At this point, he starts to cough a little, closes his eyes again, and stops talking. I can't believe the first thing he wants to plan is a new club based on the explorations of Charles Darwin. Haven't we had enough of this guy?

"Wasn't it Darwin who talked about natural selection?" I ask, feeling foolish because Andrew's lying in a hospital bed in what looks like a girl's nightgown and I'm talking to him about some crazy scientist who died over a hundred years ago. "Didn't he write about how those members of each species that are best adapted to their environment are the ones who live and procreate?"

It takes a minute before Andrew answers.

"Procreate?" he says, opening one eye and fixing it on me.

All of a sudden it hits me. Without the Annelid club, I would never have given Darwin or his theories a second thought. Andrew wouldn't have had a chance to form the club and teach us all about worms and what they mean to the earth. And my brother, my big, beautiful, stupid brother, would not have

121

realized there are lines you shouldn't cross, things you shouldn't do, and that loving your little brother isn't such a bad thing after all. The biggest surprise, though, is that I now know how to use words like procreate.

I lower my forehead down against the side of his bed and let out this giant moan, and then I look up at him and start to laugh. Andrew opens his eyes and joins in, weak at first, then stronger. The two of us are still cracking up when the curtain sweeps to one side and a startled nurse arrives to take his temperature.

"Hold on a second," I tell her and lean forward so I can say something to Andrew before I go. "This is important. Who said, 'A man's friendships are one of the best measures of his worth'?"

Andrew looks at me as if I'm crazy. For a second he says nothing while the nurse rips open the thermometer bag.

"You got me," he says. "Who?"

"Your man Darwin."

I only know this because I looked him up on the Internet.

Andrew closes his eyes again, rests his head back against the pillow, and smiles.

"Excellent, Wills," he manages to say before the nurse pops the thermometer under his tongue and he can speak no more.

# About the Author

Lucia Greene grew up by a river in Connecticut, lived by the harbor in South Freeport, Maine, and finished her childhood on a farm in Poland Spring, Maine. A lifelong reader and writer, she edited children's books, had a career as a journalist for *People* Magazine, and is currently a freelance writer. She and her husband have three grown children and live in Newburyport, Massachusetts.